A

CHILD'S
ANTHOLOGY

OF

POETRY

A
CHILD'S
ANTHOLOGY
OF
POETRY

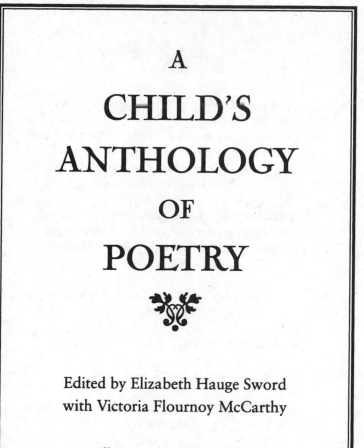

Edited by Elizabeth Hauge Sword
with Victoria Flournoy McCarthy

Illustrated by Tom Pohrt

ecco
An Imprint of HarperCollins*Publishers*

Printed in the United States of America. No part
of this book may be used or reproduced in any manner what-
soever without written permission except in the case of brief
quotations embodied in critical articles and review. For
information address HarperCollins Publishers, 195 Broadway,
New York, NY 10007.

HarperCollins books may be purchased for educational,
business, or sales promotional use. For information please
e-mail the Special Markets Department at SPsales@
harpercollins.com

A hardcover edition of this book was published in 2006 by Ecco,
an imprint of HarperCollins Publishers.

FIRST ECCO PAPERBACK EDITION PUBLISHED IN 2015.

Designed by Debby Jay Book Design

The Library of Congress has cataloged the hardcover edition
as follows:

Library of Congress Cataloging in Publication Data
A child's anthology of poetry / edited by Elizabeth Hauge Sword
with Victoria Flournoy McCarthy ; illustrated by Tom Pohrt.
        p.   cm.
            ISBN 0-88001-378-8
1.   Children's poetry.   I.   Sword, Elizabeth Hauge.
        II.   McCarthy, Victoria.
            PN1058.C52   1995
        808.81'0083   dc20   95-15742

Page 313 consitutes an extension of this page.

The text of this book was set in Sabon.

ISBN 978-0-06-239337-1

23 24 25 26 27 LBC 10 9 8 7 6

For my children—

PAYSON, BAYLESS, AND MORGAN

*a volume filled with
memories to come*

CONTENTS

INTRODUCTION

When my son was in second grade, he was asked to share a poem with his class each month. In searching through bookstores and libraries, however, we were unable to find an anthology that offered a range of fine poetry within the grasp of an elementary school student. What was missing was a volume that awakened a young reader to the excitement, the beauty, the power and the fun of poetry.

A Child's Anthology of Poetry challenges the notion that a child's ability to enjoy and appreciate poetry is limited. It celebrates poetry while respecting its intended audience. We have included classic poems we loved as children, poems we memorized and contemporary poems we have discovered with our children. A few of these selections will challenge young readers, but they are too valuable to omit.

It is our hope that parents, grandparents, aunts, uncles, teachers and good friends will take the time to read the poems aloud with the special children in their lives. For a child to hear "Paul Revere's Ride" or "Mother to Son" adds another dimension to the poem and creates a shared experience that goes far beyond the printed page. At a time in our children's lives when they commit so much to memory, so effortlessly, exposure to poetry, and its later remembrance, can bring a lifetime of enjoyment.

We chose to organize this collection alphabetically by author. This format makes the book more accessible to teachers using the anthology as a text and to browsers hunting for their favorite poems.

I would like to thank the advisory board members for their important recommendations. Their wisdom and experience are in large measure responsible for the extraordinary body of poetry assembled here. Tom Pohrt's artwork brings additional beauty to the collection. My thanks also to Dan and Jeanne Halpern who agreed from the outset that children (and grownups) needed this book; their vision has enriched this collection. To all members of my family, my friends and colleagues who shared their list of favorites with me, I am ever grateful. A special thanks to Jay for sharing his remarkable artistic talent. Most importantly, to Vickie, my profound appreciation for her friendship and unfailing support throughout the life of this project.

I hope this book opens "magic casements" for everyone who reads these poems. Whether a child's interest lies in a poem's words, story, rhythm or rhyme, poetry can foster a lifelong love of language. This is a gift beyond measure.

ELIZABETH HAUGE SWORD

A

CHILD'S
ANTHOLOGY
OF
POETRY

Hiding

I'm hiding, I'm hiding,
And no one knows where;
For all they can see is my
Toes and my hair.

And I just heard my father
Say to my mother—
"But, darling, he must be
Somewhere or other;

Have you looked in the inkwell?"
And Mother said, "Where?"
"In the INKWELL?" said Father. But
I was not there.

Then "Wait!" cried my mother—
"I think that I see
Him under the carpet." But
It was not me.

"Inside the mirror's
A pretty good place,"
Said Father and looked, but saw
Only his face.

"We've hunted," sighed Mother,
"As hard as we could
And I AM so afraid that we've
Lost him for good."

Then I laughed out aloud
And I wiggled my toes
And Father said—"Look, dear,
I wonder if those

Toes could be Benny's?
There are ten of them, see?"
And they WERE so surprised to find
Out it was me!

—DOROTHY ALDIS

The Creation

All things bright and beautiful,
    All creatures, great and small,
All things wise and wonderful,
    The Lord God made them all.

Each little flower that opens,
    Each little bird that sings,
He made their glowing colors,
    He made their tiny wings;

The rich man in his castle,
    The poor man at his gate,
God made them, high or lowly,
    And ordered their estate.

The purple-headed mountain,
    The river running by,
The sunset and the morning,
    That brightens up the sky;

The cold wind in the winter,
    The pleasant summer sun,
The ripe fruits in the garden—
    He made them every one.

The tall trees in the greenwood,
    The meadows where we play,
The rushes by the water
    We gather every day,—

He gave us eyes to see them,
    And lips that we might tell
How great is God Almighty,
    Who has made all things well!

—CECIL FRANCIS ALEXANDER

Life Doesn't Frighten Me

Shadows on the wall
Noises down the hall
Life doesn't frighten me at all
Bad dogs barking loud
Big ghosts in a cloud
Life doesn't frighten me at all.
Mean old Mother Goose
Lions on the loose
They don't frighten me at all
Dragons breathing flame
On my counterpane
That doesn't frighten me at all.
I go boo
Make them shoo
I make fun
Way they run
I won't cry
So they fly
I just smile
They go wild
Life doesn't frighten me at all.
Tough guys fight
All alone at night
Life doesn't frighten me at all.
Panthers in the park
Strangers in the dark
No, they don't frighten me at all.
That new classroom where
Boys all pull my hair
(Kissy little girls
With their hair in curls)
They don't frighten me at all.
Don't show me frogs and snakes
And listen for my scream,
If I'm afraid at all
It's only in my dreams.
I've got a magic charm
That I keep up my sleeve,

I can walk the ocean floor
And never have to breathe.
Life doesn't frighten me at all
 Not at all
 Not at all.
Life doesn't frighten me at all.

—MAYA ANGELOU

Song for a Young Girl's Puberty Ceremony

I am on my way running,
I am on my way running,
Looking toward me is the edge of the world,
I am trying to reach it,
The edge of the world does not look far away,
To that I am on my way running.

—ANONYMOUS

Translated by
Frances Densmore

Song for the Sun That Disappeared
behind the Rainclouds

The fire darkens, the wood turns black.
The flame extinguishes, misfortune upon us.
God sets out in search of the sun.
The rainbow sparkles in his hand,
The bow of the divine hunter.
He has heard the lamentations of his children.
He walks along the milky way, he collects the stars.
With quick arms he piles them into a basket
Piles them up with quick arms
Like a woman who collects lizards
And piles them into her pot, piles them
Until the pot overflows with lizards
Until the basket overflows with light.

—ANONYMOUS

A Visit from Mr. Fox

The Fox set out in hungry plight,
 And begged the moon to give him light,
For he'd many a mile to travel that night,
 Before he could reach his den, O!

First he came to a farmer's yard,
 Where the ducks and geese declared it was hard
That their nerves should be shaken, and their rest be marred
 By a visit from Mr. Fox, O!

He seized the gray goose by the sleeve,
 Says he, "Madame Gray Goose, by your leave,
I'll carry you off without reprieve,
 And take you away to my den, O!"

He seized the gray duck by the neck,
 And flung her over across his back,
While the old duck cried out, "Quack, quack, quack!"
 With her legs dangling down behind, O!

Then old Mrs. Flipper Flapper jumped out of bed,
 And out of the window she popped her head,
Crying, "John, John, John, the gray goose is gone,
 And the Fox is off to his den, O!"

Then John went up to the top of the hill,
 And he blew a blast both loud and shrill.
Says the Fox, "That is fine music, still
 I'd rather be off to my den, O!"

So the Fox he hurried home to his den,
 To his dear little foxes eight, nine, ten.
"We're in luck, here's a big fat duck
 With her legs dangling down behind, O!"

The Fox sat down with his hungry wife,
    And they made a good meal without fork or knife.
They never had a better time in all their life,
    And the little ones picked the bones, O!

—ANONYMOUS

Do you carrot all for me?

Do you carrot all for me?
My heart beets for you,
With your turnip nose
And your radish face,
You are a peach.
If we cantaloupe,
Lettuce marry;
Weed make a swell pear.

—ANONYMOUS

Monday's Child Is Fair of Face

Monday's child is fair of face,
Tuesday's child is full of grace,
Wednesday's child is full of woe,
Thursday's child has far to go,
Friday's child is loving and giving,
Saturday's child works hard for a living,
And the child that is born on the Sabbath day
Is bonny and blithe, and good and gay.

—ANONYMOUS

Mr. Nobody

I know a funny little man,
    As quiet as a mouse,
Who does the mischief that is done
    In everybody's house!
There's no one ever sees his face,
    And yet we all agree
That every plate we break was cracked
    By Mr. Nobody.

'Tis he who always tears our books,
    Who leaves the door ajar,
He pulls the buttons from our shirts,
    And scatters pins afar;
That squeaking door will always squeak,
    For, prithee, don't you see,
We leave the oiling to be done
    By Mr. Nobody.

The finger marks upon the door
    By none of us are made;
We never leave the blinds unclosed,
    To let the curtains fade.
The ink we never spill; the boots
    That lying round you see
Are not our boots—they all belong
    To Mr. Nobody.

—ANONYMOUS

I Shall Not Pass This Way Again

Through this toilsome world, alas!
Once and only once I pass;
If a kindness I may show,
If a good deed I may do
To a suffering fellow man,
Let me do it while I can.
No delay, for it is plain
I shall not pass this way again.

—ANONYMOUS

Somebody's Mother

The woman was old, and ragged, and gray,
And bent with the chill of the winter's day;

The street was wet with a recent snow,
And the woman's feet were aged and slow.

She stood at the crossing and waited long,
Alone, uncared for, amid the throng

Of human beings who passed her by,
Nor heeded the glance of her anxious eye.

Down the street, with laughter and shout,
Glad in the freedom of "school let out,"

Came the boys like a flock of sheep,
Hailing the snow piled white and deep.

Past the woman so old and gray
Hastened the children on their way,

Nor offered a helping hand to her—
So meek, so timid, afraid to stir

Lest the carriage wheels or the horses' feet
Should crowd her down in the slippery street.

At last came one of the merry troop—
The gayest laddie of all the group;

He paused beside her and whispered low,
"I'll help you across if you wish to go."

Her aged hand on his strong young arm
She placed, and so, without hurt or harm,

He guided the trembling feet along,
Proud that his own were firm and strong.

Then back again to his friends he went,
His young heart happy and well content.

"She's somebody's mother, boys, you know,
For all she's aged and poor and slow;

"And I hope some fellow will lend a hand
To help my mother, you understand,

"If ever she's poor and old and gray,
When her own dear boy is far away."

And "somebody's mother" bowed low her head
In her home that night and the prayer she said

Was, "God, be kind to the noble boy
Who is somebody's son and pride and joy!"

—ANONYMOUS

The Cats of Kilkenny

There were once two cats of Kilkenny,
Each thought there was one cat too many;
So they fought and they fit,
And they scratched and they bit,
Till, excepting their nails
And the tips of their tails,
Instead of two cats, there weren't any.

—ANONYMOUS

The Cowboy's Lament

As I walked out in the streets of Laredo,
As I walked out in Laredo one day,
I spied a poor cowboy wrapped up in white linen,
Wrapped up in white linen as cold as the clay.

"Oh, beat the drum slowly and play the fife lowly,
Play the dead march as you carry me along;
Take me to the green valley, there lay the sod o'er me,
For I'm a young cowboy and I know I've done wrong.

"It was once in the saddle I used to go dashing,
It was once in the saddle I used to go gay;
First to the dram-house and then to the card-house;
Got shot in the breast and I'm dying today.

"Get six jolly cowboys to carry my coffin;
Get six pretty maidens to bear up my pall.
Put bunches of roses all over my coffin,
Put roses to deaden the sods as they fall.

"Then swing your rope slowly and rattle your spurs lowly,
And give a wild whoop as you carry me along;
And in the grave throw me and roll the sod o'er me
For I'm a young cowboy and I know I've done wrong."

We beat the drum slowly and played the fife lowly,
And bitterly wept as we bore him along;
For we all loved our comrade, so brave, young, and handsome,
We all loved our comrade although he'd done wrong.

—ANONYMOUS

Good Sportsmanship

Good sportsmanship we hail, we sing,
    It's always pleasant when you spot it.
There's only one unhappy thing:
    You have to lose to prove you've got it.

                   —RICHARD ARMOUR

Pachycephalosaurus

Among the later dinosaurs
    Though not the largest, strongest,
PACHYCEPHALOSAURUS had
    The name that was the longest.

Yet he had more than syllables,
    As you may well suppose.
He had great knobs upon his cheeks
    And spikes upon his nose.

Ten inches thick, atop his head,
    A bump of bone projected.
By this his brain, though hardly worth
    Protecting, was protected.

No claw or tooth, no tree that fell
    Upon his head kerwhacky,
Could crack or crease or jar or scar
    That stony part of Paky.

And so he nibbled plants in peace
    And lived untroubled days.
Sometimes, in fact, as Paky proved,
    To be a bonehead pays.

                —RICHARD ARMOUR

Song Form

Morning uptown, quiet on the street,
no matter the distinctions that can be
made, quiet, very quiet, on the street.
Sun's not even up, just some kid and me,
skating, both of us, at the early sun, and
amazed there is grace for us, without our
having to smile too tough, or be very pleasant
even to each other. Merely to be mere, ly to be

—AMIRI BARAKA

It would melt
in my hand—
the autumn frost.
—BASHŌ MATSUO

The old pond—
a frog jumps in,
plop!
—BASHŌ MATSUO

The Frog

Be kind and tender to the Frog,
    And do not call him names,
As "Slimy-skin," or "Polly-wog,"
    Or likewise "Uncle James,"
Or "Gape-a-grin," or "Toad-gone-wrong,"
    Or "Billy Bandy-knees":
The frog is justly sensitive
    To epithets like these.

No animal will more repay
    A treatment kind and fair,
At least, so lonely people say
Who keep a frog (and by the way,
    They are extremely rare).

—HILAIRE BELLOC

The Witch of Willowby Wood

There once was a witch of Willowby Wood,
and a weird wild witch was she, with hair that was snarled
and hands that were gnarled, and a kickety, rickety
knee. She could jump, they say,
to the moon and back, but this I never did see.
Now Willowby Wood was near Sassafras Swamp,
where there's never a road or rut. And there by the
singing witch-hazel bush the old woman builded
her hut. She builded with neither a hammer or shovel. She
kneaded, she rolled out, she baked
her brown hovel. For all witches' houses, I've oft heard
it said, are made of stick candy and fresh
gingerbread. But the shingles that shingled this old
witch's roof were lollipop shingles and hurricane-proof,
　　　too
hard to be pelted and melted by rain.
(Why this is important, I soon will explain.)
One day there came running to Sassafras Swamp a dark little
shadowy mouse. He was noted for being a scoundrel
and scamp. And he gnawed at the old woman's house
　　　where the
doorpost was weak and the doorpost was worn.
And when the witch scolded, he laughed her to scorn.
And when the witch chased him, he felt quite delighted.
　　　She
never could catch him for she was nearsighted. And so,
though she quibbled, he gnawed and he nibbled.
The witch said, "I won't have my house
take a tumble. I'll search in my magical book for a spell
I can weave and a charm I can mumble to get you
away from this nook. It will be a good warning to other
bad mice, who won't earn their bread
but go stealing a slice."
"Your charms cannot hurt," said the mouse, looking pert.
Well, she looked in her book and she
waved her right arm, and she said the most magical
things. Till the mouse, feeling strange,

looked about in alarm, and found he was growing some
wings. He flapped and he fluttered the longer she
                    muttered.

"And now, my fine fellow,
    you'd best be aloof," said the witch as he floundered
around. "You can't stay on earth and you
can't gnaw my roof. It's lollipop-hard and it's
hurricane-proof. So you'd better take off
from the ground. If you are wise, stay in the skies."
Then in went the woman of Willowby Wood,
in to her hearthstone and cat.
There she put her old volume up high on the shelf, and
fanned her hot face with her hat. Then she said,
"That is *that!* I have just made a *bat!*"

—ROWENA BENNETT

The Gingerbread Man

The gingerbread man gave a gingery shout:
"Quick! Open the oven and let me out!"
He stood up straight in his baking pan.
He jumped to the floor and away he ran.
"Catch me," he called, "if you can, can, can."

The gingerbread man met a cock and a pig
And a dog that was brown and twice as big
As himself. But he called to them all as he ran,
"You can't catch a runaway gingerbread man."

The gingerbread man met a reaper and sower.
The gingerbread man met a thresher and mower;
But no matter how fast they scampered and ran
They couldn't catch up with a gingerbread man.

Then he came to a fox and he turned to face him.
He dared Old Reynard to follow and chase him;
But when he stepped under the fox's nose
Something happened. What do you s'pose?
The fox gave a snap. The fox gave a yawn,
And the gingerbread man was gone, gone, GONE.

—ROWENA BENNETT

The Ball Poem

What is the boy now, who has lost his ball,
What, what is he to do? I saw it go
Merrily bouncing, down the street, and then
Merrily over—there it is in the water!
No use to say "O there are other balls":
An ultimate shaking grief fixes the boy
As he stands rigid, trembling, staring down
All his young days into the harbour where
His ball went. I would not intrude on him,
A dime, another ball, is worthless. Now
He senses first responsibility
In a world of possessions. People will take balls,
Balls will be lost always, little boy,
And no one buys a ball back. Money is external.
He is learning, well behind his desperate eyes,
The epistemology of loss, how to stand up
Knowing what every man must one day know
And most know many days, how to stand up.
And gradually light returns to the street,
A whistle blows, the ball is out of sight,
Soon part of me will explore the deep and dark
Floor of the harbour . . . I am everywhere,
I suffer and move, my mind and my heart move
With all that move me, under the water
Or whistling, I am not a little boy.

—JOHN BERRYMAN

The Fish

I caught a tremendous fish
and held him beside the boat
half out of water, with my hook
fast in a corner of his mouth.
He didn't fight.
He hadn't fought at all.
He hung a grunting weight,
battered and venerable
and homely. Here and there
his brown skin hung in strips
like ancient wallpaper,
and its pattern of darker brown
was like wallpaper:
shapes like full-blown roses
stained and lost through age.
He was speckled with barnacles,
fine rosettes of lime,
and infested
with tiny white sea-lice,
and underneath two or three
rags of green weed hung down.
While his gills were breathing in
the terrible oxygen
—the frightening gills,
fresh and crisp with blood,
that can cut so badly—
I thought of the coarse white flesh
packed in like feathers,
the big bones and the little bones,
the dramatic reds and blacks
of his shiny entrails,
and the pink swim-bladder
like a big peony.
I looked into his eyes
which were far larger than mine
but shallower, and yellowed,
the irises backed and packed
with tarnished tinfoil

seen through the lenses
of old scratched isinglass.
They shifted a little, but not
to return my stare.
—It was more like the tipping
of an object toward the light.
I admired his sullen face,
the mechanism of his jaw,
and then I saw
that from his lower lip
—if you could call it a lip—
grim, wet, and weaponlike,
hung five old pieces of fish-line,
or four and a wire leader
with the swivel still attached,
with all their five big hooks
grown firmly in his mouth.
A green line, frayed at the end
where he broke it, two heavier lines,
and a fine black thread
still crimped from the strain and snap
when it broke and he got away.
Like medals with their ribbons
frayed and wavering,
a five-haired beard of wisdom
trailing from his aching jaw.
I stared and stared
and victory filled up
the little rented boat,
from the pool of bilge
where oil had spread a rainbow
around the rusted engine
to the bailer rusted orange,
the sun-cracked thwarts,
the oarlocks on their strings,
the gunnels—until everything
was rainbow, rainbow, rainbow!
And I let the fish go.

—ELIZABETH BISHOP

Cirque d'Hiver

Across the floor flits the mechanical toy,
fit for a king of several centuries back.
A little circus horse with real white hair.
His eyes are glossy black.
He bears a little dancer on his back.

She stands upon her toes and turns and turns.
A slanting spray of artificial roses
is stitched across her skirt and tinsel bodice.
Above her head she poses
another spray of artificial roses.

His mane and tail are straight from Chirico.
He has a formal, melancholy soul.
He feels her pink toes dangle toward his back
along the little pole
that pierces both her body and her soul

and goes through his, and reappears below,
under his belly, as a big tin key.
He canters three steps, then he makes a bow,
canters again, bows on one knee,
canters, then clicks and stops, and looks at me.

The dancer, by this time, has turned her back.
He is the more intelligent by far.
Facing each other rather desperately—
his eye is like a star—
we stare and say, "Well, we have come this far."

—ELIZABETH BISHOP

Sestina

September rain falls on the house.
In the failing light, the old grandmother
sits in the kitchen with the child
beside the Little Marvel Stove,
reading the jokes from the almanac,
laughing and talking to hide her tears.

She thinks that her equinoctial tears
and the rain that beats on the roof of the house
were both foretold by the almanac,
but only known to a grandmother.
The iron kettle sings on the stove.
She cuts some bread and says to the child,

It's time for tea now; but the child
is watching the teakettle's small hard tears
dance like mad on the hot black stove,
the way the rain must dance on the house.
Tidying up, the old grandmother
hangs up the clever almanac

on its string. Birdlike, the almanac
hovers half open above the child,
hovers above the old grandmother
and her teacup full of dark brown tears.
She shivers and says she thinks the house
feels chilly, and puts more wood in the stove.

It was to be, says the Marvel Stove.
I know what I know, says the almanac.
With crayons the child draws a rigid house
and a winding pathway. Then the child
puts in a man with buttons like tears
and shows it proudly to the grandmother.

But secretly, while the grandmother
busies herself about the stove,

the little moons fall down like tears
from between the pages of the almanac
into the flower bed the child
has carefully placed in the front of the house.

Time to plant tears, says the almanac.
The grandmother sings to the marvelous stove
and the child draws another inscrutable house.

—ELIZABETH BISHOP

Piping down the Valleys

Piping down the valleys wild,
     Piping songs of pleasant glee,
On a cloud I saw a child,
     And he laughing said to me:

"Pipe a song about a Lamb!"
     So I piped with merry cheer.
"Piper, pipe that song again!"
     So I piped; he wept to hear.

"Drop thy pipe, thy happy pipe;
     Sing thy songs of happy cheer!"
So I sang the same again,
     While he wept with joy to hear.

"Piper, sit thee down and write
     In a book, that all may read."
So he vanished from my sight.
     And I plucked a hollow reed

And I made a rural pen,
     And I stained the water clear,
And I wrote my happy songs
     Every child may joy to hear.

          —WILLIAM BLAKE

The Shepherd

How sweet is the Shepherd's sweet lot!
From the morn to the evening he strays;
He shall follow his sheep all the day,
And his tongue shall be filled with praise.

For he hears the lamb's innocent call,
And he hears the ewe's tender reply;
He is watchful while they are in peace,
For they know when their Shepherd is nigh.

—WILLIAM BLAKE

The Tyger

Tyger! Tyger! burning bright
In the forests of the night,
What immortal hand or eye
Could frame thy fearful symmetry?

In what distant deeps or skies
Burnt the fire of thine eyes?
On what wings dare he aspire?
What the hand dare seize the fire?

And what shoulder, and what art,
Could twist the sinews of thy heart?
And, when thy heart began to beat,
What dread hand? and what dread feet?

What the hammer? what the chain?
In what furnace was thy brain?
What the anvil? what dread grasp
Dare its deadly terrors clasp?

When the stars threw down their spears,
And watered heaven with their tears,
Did he smile his work to see?
Did he who made the lamb make thee?

Tyger! Tyger! burning bright
In the forests of the night,
What immortal hand or eye,
Dare frame thy fearful symmetry?

—WILLIAM BLAKE

The Little Black Boy

My mother bore me in the southern wild,
And I am black, but O! my soul is white;
White as an angel is the English child,
But I am black, as if bereav'd of light.

My mother taught me underneath a tree,
And sitting down before the heat of day,
She took me on her lap and kissed me,
And pointing to the east, began to say:

"Look on the rising sun: there God does live,
And gives his light, and gives his heat away;
And flowers and trees and beasts and man receive
Comfort in morning, joy in the noonday.

"And we are put on earth a little space,
That we may learn to bear the beams of love;
And these black bodies and this sunburnt face
Is but a cloud, and like a shady grove.

"For when our souls have learn'd that heat to bear,
The cloud will vanish; we shall hear his voice,
Saying: 'Come out from the grove, my love & care,
And round my golden tent like lambs rejoice.'"

Thus did my mother say, and kissed me;
And thus I say to the little English boy:
When I from black and he from white cloud free,
And round the tent of God like lambs we joy,

I'll shade him from the heat, till he can bear
To lean in joy upon our father's knee;
And then I'll stand and stroke his silver hair,
And be like him, and he will then love me.

—WILLIAM BLAKE

The Divine Image

To Mercy, Pity, Peace, and Love
All pray in their distress;
And to these virtues of delight
Return their thankfulness.

For Mercy, Pity, Peace, and Love
Is God, our father dear,
And Mercy, Pity, Peace, and Love
Is Man, his child and care.

For Mercy has a human heart,
Pity a human face,
And Love, the human form divine,
And Peace, the human dress.

Then every man, of every clime,
That prays in his distress,
Prays to the human form divine,
Love, Mercy, Pity, Peace.

And all must love the human form,
In heathen, turk, or jew;
Where Mercy, Love, & Pity dwell
There God is dwelling too.

—WILLIAM BLAKE

spring equinox

Now day and night sit balanced.
From a silence that seemed forever,
the first booming crash of break-up
thunders from the river. Smiling,
      an elder oils the handle of a hoe
and listens for that great, warm wind.

Creation is a song, a trickling become
a gurgling, chuckling water voice.
Winds which bend the snows to melting
carry clouds of rain storms on shoulder.
      Green islands appear on turtle's back
grasses long asleep beneath the snow.

Dawn of a glorious season, flowers
in merging, undulating waves of color
The taste of strawberries, anticipate
in their blossoms, the rich and fertile
      smells of soil we bend to,
breaking the ground for summer's corn.

—PETER BLUE CLOUD

Hunchback Girl: She Thinks of Heaven

My Father, it is surely a blue place
And straight. Right. Regular. Where I shall find
No need for scholarly nonchalance or looks
A little to the left or guards upon the
Heart to halt love that runs without crookedness
Along its crooked corridors. My Father,
It is a planned place, surely. Out of coils,
Unscrewed, released, no more to be marvelous,
I shall walk straightly through most proper halls
Proper myself, princess of properness.

—GWENDOLYN BROOKS

A Red, Red Rose

O, my love is like a red, red rose,
    That's newly sprung in June:
O, my love is like the melody
    That's sweetly play'd in tune.

As fair art thou, my bonnie lass,
    So deep in love am I,
And I will love thee still, my dear,
    Till all the seas gang dry.

Till all the seas gang dry, my dear,
    And the rocks melt wi' the sun!
And I will love thee still, my dear,
    While the sands o' life shall run.

And fare thee well, my only love,
    And fare thee well a while!
And I will come again, my love,
    Tho' it were ten thousand mile!

—ROBERT BURNS

My heart's in the Highlands,
my heart is not here

My heart's in the Highlands, my heart is not here;
My heart's in the Highlands a-chasing the deer;
Chasing the wild deer, and following the roe,
My heart's in the Highlands wherever I go.
Farewell to the Highlands, farewell to the North,
The birth-place of valour, the country of worth;
Wherever I wander, wherever I rove,
The hills of the Highlands for ever I love.

Farewell to the mountains, high covered with snow;
Farewell to the straths and green valleys below;
Farewell to the forests and wild-hanging woods;
Farewell to the torrents and loud-pouring floods.
My heart's in the Highlands, my heart is not here;
My heart's in the Highlands a-chasing the deer;
Chasing the wild deer, and following the roe,
My heart's in the Highlands, wherever I go.

—ROBERT BURNS

A tethered horse,
snow
in both stirrups.

—YOSA BUSON

I go,
you stay;
two autumns.

—YOSA BUSON

That snail—
one long horn, one short,
what's on his mind?

—YOSA BUSON

The Destruction of Sennacherib

The Assyrian came down like the wolf on the fold,
And his cohorts were gleaming in purple and gold;
And the sheen of their spears was like stars on the sea,
When the blue wave rolls nightly on deep Galilee.

Like the leaves of the forest when Summer is green,
That host with their banners at sunset were seen:
Like the leaves of the forest when Autumn hath flown,
That host on the morrow lay withered and strown.

For the Angel of Death spread his wings on the blast,
And breathed in the face of the foe as he passed;
And the eyes of the sleepers waxed deadly and chill,
And their hearts but once heaved, and forever grew still.

And there lay the steed with his nostril all wide,
But through it there rolled not the breath of his pride;
And the foam of his gasping lay white on the turf,
And cold as the spray of the rock-beating surf.

And there lay the rider distorted and pale,
With the dew on his brow, and the rust on his mail;
And the tents were all silent, the banners alone,
The lances unlifted, the trumpet unblown.

And the widows of Ashur are loud in their wail,
And the idols are broke in the temple of Baal;
And the might of the Gentile, unsmote by the sword,
Hath melted like snow in the glance of the Lord!

—GEORGE GORDON, LORD BYRON

So, We'll Go No More a Roving

So, we'll go no more a roving
        So late into the night,
Though the heart be still as loving,
        And the moon be still as bright.

For the sword outwears its sheath,
        And the soul wears out the breast,
And the heart must pause to breathe,
        And love itself have rest.

Though the night was made for loving,
        And the day returns too soon,
Yet we'll go no more a roving
        By the light of the moon.

—GEORGE GORDON, LORD BYRON

The Castle in the Fire

The andirons were the dragons,
    Set out to guard the gate
Of the old enchanted castle,
    In the fire upon the grate.

We saw a turret window
    Open a little space,
And frame, for just a moment,
    A lady's lovely face;

Then, while we watched in wonder
    From out the smoky veil,
A gallant knight came riding,
    Dressed in coat of mail;

With slender lance a-tilting,
    Thrusting with a skillful might,
He charged the crouching dragons—
    Ah, 'twas a brilliant fight!

Then, in the roar and tumult,
    The back log crashed in two,
And castle, knight and dragons
    Were hidden from our view;

But, when the smoke had lifted,
    We saw, to our delight,
Riding away together,
    The lady and the knight.

—MARY JANE CARR

The Crocodile

How doth the little crocodile
    Improve his shining tail,
And pour the waters of the Nile
    On every golden scale!

How cheerfully he seems to grin!
    How neatly spread his claws,
And welcomes little fishes in
    With gently smiling jaws!

—LEWIS CARROLL

Father William

"You are old, Father William," the young man said,
"And your hair has become very white;
  And yet you incessantly stand on your head—
  Do you think, at your age, it is right?"

  "In my youth," Father William replied to his son,
  "I feared it might injure the brain;
    But now that I'm perfectly sure I have none,
    Why, I do it again and again."

"You are old," said the youth, "as I mentioned before,
And have grown most uncommonly fat;
  Yet you turn a back somersault in at the door—
  Pray, what is the reason for that?"

  "In my youth," said the sage, as he shook his gray locks,
  "I kept all my limbs very supple
    By the use of this ointment—one shilling the box—
    Allow me to sell you a couple?"

"You are old," said the youth, "and your jaws are too weak
For anything tougher than suet;
  Yet you finished the goose, with the bones and the beak—
  Pray, how did you manage to do it?"

  "In my youth," said his father, "I took to the law,
  And argued each case with my wife;
    And the muscular strength which it gave to my jaw
    Has lasted the rest of my life."

"You are old," said the youth; "one would hardly suppose
That your eye was as steady as ever;
  Yet you balanced an eel on the end of your nose—
  What made you so awfully clever?"

"I have answered three questions, and that is enough,"
Said his father. "Don't give yourself airs!
Do you think I can listen all day to such stuff?
Be off, or I'll kick you downstairs!"

—LEWIS CARROLL

Jabberwocky

'Twas brillig, and the slithy toves
    Did gyre and gimble in the wabe:
All mimsy were the borogoves,
    And the mome raths outgrabe.

"Beware the Jabberwock, my son!
    The jaws that bite, the claws that catch!
Beware the Jubjub bird, and shun
    The frumious Bandersnatch!"

He took his vorpal sword in hand:
    Long time the manxome foe he sought—
So rested he by the Tumtum tree,
    And stood awhile in thought.

And, as in uffish thought he stood,
    The Jabberwock, with eyes of flame,
Came whiffling through the tulgey wood,
    And burbled as it came!

One, two! One, two! And through and through
    The vorpal blade went snicker-snack!
He left it dead, and with its head
    He went galumphing back.

"And hast thou slain the Jabberwock?
    Come to my arms, my beamish boy!
O frabjous day! Callooh! Callay!"
    He chortled in his joy.

'Twas brillig, and the slithy toves
    Did gyre and gimble in the wabe:
All mimsy were the borogoves,
    And the mome raths outgrabe.

—LEWIS CARROLL

The Walrus and the Carpenter

The sun was shining on the sea,
  Shining with all his might:
He did his very best to make
  The billows smooth and bright—
And this was odd, because it was
  The middle of the night.

The moon was shining sulkily,
  Because she thought the sun
Had got no business to be there
  After the day was done—
"It's very rude of him," she said,
  "To come and spoil the fun!"

The sea was wet as wet could be,
  The sands were dry as dry,
You could not see a cloud, because
  No cloud was in the sky:
No birds were flying overhead—
  There were no birds to fly.

The Walrus and the Carpenter
  Were walking close at hand:
They wept like anything to see
  Such quantities of sand:
"If this were only cleared away,"
  They said, "it *would* be grand!"

"If seven maids with seven mops
  Swept it for half a year,
Do you suppose," the Walrus said,
  "That they could get it clear?"
"I doubt it," said the Carpenter,
  And shed a bitter tear.

"O, Oysters, come and walk with us!"
  The Walrus did beseech.
"A pleasant talk, a pleasant walk,

Along the briny beach:
We cannot do with more than four,
To give a hand to each."

The eldest Oyster looked at him,
But never a word he said;
The eldest Oyster winked his eye,
And shook his heavy head—
Meaning to say he did not choose
To leave the oyster-bed.

But four young Oysters hurried up,
All eager for the treat:
Their coats were brushed, their faces washed,
Their shoes were clean and neat—
And this was odd, because, you know,
They hadn't any feet.

Four other Oysters followed them,
And yet another four;
And thick and fast they came at last,
And more, and more, and more—
All hopping through the frothy waves,
And scrambling to the shore.

The Walrus and the Carpenter
Walked on a mile or so,
And then they rested on a rock
Conveniently low:
And all the little Oysters stood
And waited in a row.

"The time has come," the Walrus said,
"To talk of many things:
Of shoes—and ships—and sealing-wax—
Of cabbages—and kings—
And why the sea is boiling hot—
And whether pigs have wings."

"But wait a bit," the Oysters cried,
    "Before we have our chat;
For some of us are out of breath,
    And all of us are fat!"
"No hurry!" said the Carpenter.
    They thanked him much for that.

"A loaf of bread," the walrus said,
    "Is what we chiefly need:
Pepper and vinegar besides
    Are very good indeed—
Now, if you're ready, Oysters dear,
    We can begin to feed."

"But not on us!" the Oysters cried,
    Turning a little blue.
"After such kindness, that would be
    A dismal thing to do!"
"The night is fine," the Walrus said.
    "Do you admire the view?

"It was so kind of you to come!
    And you are very nice!"
The Carpenter said nothing but
    "Cut us another slice.
I wish you were not quite so deaf—
    I've had to ask you twice!"

"It seems a shame," the Walrus said,
    "To play them such a trick,
After we've brought them out so far,
    And made them trot so quick!"
The Carpenter said nothing but
    "The butter's spread too thick!"

"I weep for you," the Walrus said:
    "I deeply sympathize."
With sobs and tears he sorted out

Those of the largest size,
Holding his pocket-handkerchief
Before his streaming eyes.

"O, Oysters," said the Carpenter,
"You've had a pleasant run!
Shall we be trotting home again?"
But answer came there none—
And this was scarcely odd, because
They'd eaten every one.

—LEWIS CARROLL

Little Trotty Wagtail

Little trotty wagtail, he went in the rain,
And twittering, tottering sideways he ne'er got straight again.
He stooped to get a worm, and looked up to get a fly,
And then he flew away ere his feathers they were dry.

Little trotty wagtail, he waddled in the mud,
And left his little footmarks, trample where he would.
He waddled in the water-pudge, and waggle went his tail,
And chirrupt up his wings to dry upon the garden rail.

Little trotty wagtail, you nimble all about,
And in the dimpling water-pudge you waddle in and out;
Your home is nigh at hand, and in the warm pig-stye,
So, little Master Wagtail, I'll bid you a good-by.

—JOHN CLARE

Swift Things Are Beautiful

Swift things are beautiful:
Swallows and deer,
And lightning that falls
Bright-veined and clear,
Rivers and meteors,
Wind in the wheat,
The strong-withered horse,
The runner's sure feet.

And slow things are beautiful:
The closing of day,
The pause of the wave
That curves downward to spray,
The ember that crumbles,
The opening flower,
And the ox that moves on
In the quiet of power.

—ELIZABETH COATSWORTH

The Garden Year

January brings the snow,
Makes our feet and fingers glow.

February brings the rain,
Thaws the frozen lake again.

March brings breezes, loud and shrill,
To stir the dancing daffodil.

April brings the primrose sweet,
Scatters daisies at our feet.

May brings flocks of pretty lambs
Skipping by their fleecy dams.

June brings tulips, lilies, roses,
Fills the children's hands with posies.

Hot July brings cooling showers,
Apricots, and gillyflowers.

August brings the sheaves of corn,
Then the harvest home is borne.

Warm September brings the fruit;
Sportsmen then begin to shoot.

Fresh October brings the pheasant;
Then to gather nuts is pleasant.

Dull November brings the blast;
Then the leaves are whirling fast.

Chill December brings the sleet,
Blazing fire, and Christmas treat.

—SARA COLERIDGE

I saw a man pursuing the horizon

I saw a man pursuing the horizon;
Round and round they sped.
I was disturbed at this;
I accosted the man.
"It is futile," I said,
"You can never—"

"You lie," he cried,
And ran on.

—STEPHEN CRANE

Incident

Once riding in Old Baltimore,
Heart filled, head filled with glee,
I saw a Baltimorean
Staring straight at me.

Now I was eight and very small,
And he was no whit bigger
And so I smiled, but he
Stuck out his tongue and called me nigger.

I saw the whole of Baltimore
From May until November.
Of all the things that happened there—
That's all that I remember.

—COUNTEE CULLEN

Heritage

What is Africa to me:
Copper sun or scarlet sea,
Jungle star or jungle track,
Strong bronzed men, or regal black
Women from whose loins I sprang
When the birds of Eden sang?
One three centuries removed
From the scenes his father loved,
Spicy grove, cinnamon tree,
What is Africa to me?

—COUNTEE CULLEN

in Just-spring

in Just-
spring   when the world is mud-
luscious the little
lame balloonman

whistles   far   and wee

and eddieandbill come
running from marbles and
piracies and it's
spring

when the world is puddle-wonderful

the queer
old balloonman whistles
far   and   wee
and bettyandisbel come dancing

from hop-scotch and jump-rope and

it's
spring
and
        the

            goat-footed

balloonman   whistles
far
and
wee

—E.E. CUMMINGS

maggie and milly and molly and may

maggie and millie and molly and may
went down to the beach(to play one day)

and maggie discovered a shell that sang
so sweetly she couldn't remember her troubles,and

milly befriended a stranded star
whose rays five languid fingers were;

and molly was chased by a horrible thing
which raced sideways while blowing bubbles:and

may came home with a smooth round stone
as small as a world and as large as alone.

For whatever we lost(like a you or a me)
it's always ourselves we find in the sea

—E.E. CUMMINGS

anyone lived in a pretty how town

anyone lived in a pretty how town
(with up so floating many bells down)
spring summer autumn winter
he sang his didn't he danced his did.

Women and men(both little and small)
cared for anyone not at all
they sowed their isn't they reaped their same
sun moon stars rain

children guessed(but only a few
and down they forgot as up they grew
autumn winter spring summer)
that noone loved him more by more

when by now and tree by leaf
she laughed his joy she cried his grief
bird by snow and stir by still
anyone's any was all to her

someones married their everyones
laughed their cryings and did their dance
(sleep wake hope and then)they
said their nevers they slept their dream

stars rain sun moon
(and only the snow can begin to explain
how children are apt to forget to remember
with up so floating many bells down)

one day anyone died i guess
(and noone stooped to kiss his face)
busy folk buried them side by side
little by little and was by was

all by all and deep by deep
and more by more they dream their sleep
noone and anyone earth by april
wish by spirit and if by yes.

Women and men(both dong and ding)
summer autumn winter spring
reaped their sowing and went their came
sun moon stars rain

—E.E. CUMMINGS

Souvenir of the Ancient World

Clara strolled in the garden with the children.
The sky was green over the grass,
the water was golden under the bridges,
other elements were blue and rose and orange,
a policeman smiled, bicycles passed,
a girl stepped onto the lawn to catch a bird,
the whole world—Germany, China—all was quiet around Clara.

The children looked at the sky: it was not forbidden.
Mouth, nose, eyes were open. There was no danger.
What Clara feared were the flu, the heat, the insects.
Clara feared missing the eleven o'clock trolley,
waiting for letters slow to arrive,
not always being able to wear a new dress. But she strolled in the
          garden, in the morning!
They had gardens, they had mornings in those days!

—CARLOS DRUMMOND DE ANDRADE
Translated by Mark Strand

Looking for Poetry

Don't write poems about what's happening.
Nothing is born or dies in poetry's presence.
Next to it, life is a static sun
without warmth or light.
Friendships, birthdays, personal matters don't count.
Don't write poems with the body,
that excellent, whole, and comfortable body objects to lyrical
        outpouring.
Your anger, your grimace of pleasure or pain in the dark
mean nothing.
Don't show off your feelings
that are slow in coming around and take advantage of doubt.
What you think and feel are not poetry yet.

Don't sing about your city, leave it in peace.
Song is not the movement of machines or the secret of houses.
It is not music heard in passing, noise of the sea in streets
        that skirt the borders of foam.
Song is not nature
or men in society.
Rain and night, fatigue and hope, mean nothing to it.
Poetry (you don't get it from things)
leaves out subject and object.

Don't dramatize, don't invoke,
don't question, don't waste time lying.
Don't get upset.
Your ivory yacht, your diamond shoe,
your mazurkas and tirades, your family skeletons,
all of them worthless, disappear in the curve of time.

Don't bring up
your sad and buried childhood.
Don't waver between the mirror
and a fading memory.
What faded was not poetry.
What broke was not crystal.

Enter the kingdom of words as if you were deaf.
Poems are there that want to be written.
They are dormant, but don't be let down,
their virginal surfaces are fresh and serene.
They are alone and mute, in dictionary condition.
Live with your poems before you write them.
If they're vague, be patient. If they offend, be calm.
Wait until each one comes into its own and demolishes
with its command of words
and its command of silence.
Don't force poems to let go of limbo.
Don't pick up lost poems from the ground.
Don't fawn over poems. Accept them
as you would their final and definitive form,
distilled in space.

Come close and consider the words.
With a plain face hiding thousands of other faces
and with no interest in your response,
whether weak or strong,
each word asks:
Did you bring the key?

Take note:
words hide in the night
in caves of music and image.
Still humid and pregnant with sleep
they turn in a winding river and by neglect are transformed.

—CARLOS DRUMMOND DE ANDRADE
Translated by Mark Strand

The Elephant

I make an elephant
from the little
I have. Wood
from old furniture
holds him up, and I fill him
with cotton, silk,
and sweetness.
Glue keeps his heavy
ears in place.
His rolled-up trunk
is the happiest part
of his architecture.
And his tusks are made
of that rare material
I cannot fake.
A white fortune
rolling around
in circus dust
without being
lost or stolen.
And finally there are
the eyes where the most
fluid and permanent
part of the elephant
stays, free of dishonesty.

Here's my poor elephant
ready to leave
to find friends
in a tired world
that no longer believes
in animals and doesn't
trust in things.
Here he is: an imposing
and fragile bulk,
who shakes his head
and moves slowly,
his hide stitched

with cloth flowers
and clouds—allusions
to a more poetic world
where love reassembles
the natural forms.

My elephant goes
down a crowded street,
but nobody looks
not even to laugh
at his tail that threatens
to leave him.
He is all grace, except
his legs don't help
and his swollen belly
will collapse
at the slightest touch.
He expresses
with elegance
his minimal life
and no one in town
is willing to take
to himself
from that tender body
the fugitive image,
the clumsy walk.

Easily moved,
he yearns for
sad situations,
unhappy people,
moonlit encounters
in the deepest ocean,
under the roots of trees,
in the bosom of shells;
he yearns for lights
that do not blind
yet shine into

the shade surrounding
the thickest trunks;
he walks the battlefield
without crushing plants,
searching for places,
secrets, stories
untold in any book,
whose style only the wind,
the leaves, the ant
recognize, but men
ignore since they dare
show themselves only
under a veiled place
and to closed eyes.

And now late at night
my elephant returns,
but returns tired out,
his shaky legs
break down in the dust.
He didn't find
what he wanted,
what we wanted,
I and my elephant,
in whom I love
to disguise myself.
Tired of searching,
his huge machinery
collapses like paper.
The paste gives way
and all his contents,
forgiveness, sweetness,
feathers, cotton,
burst out on the rug,
like a myth torn apart.
Tomorrow I begin again.

—CARLOS DRUMMOND DE ANDRADE
Translated by Mark Strand

Some One

Some one came knocking
    At my wee, small door;
Some one came knocking,
    I'm sure—sure—sure;
I listened, I opened,
    I looked to left and right,
But nought there was a-stirring
    In the still dark night;
Only the busy beetle
    Tap-tapping in the wall,
Only from the forest
    The screech-owl's call,
Only the cricket whistling
    While the dewdrops fall,
So I know not who came knocking,
    At all, at all, at all.

—WALTER DE LA MARE

The Ride-by-Nights

Up on their brooms the Witches stream,
Crooked and black in the crescent's gleam,
One foot high, and one foot low,
Bearded, cloaked, and cowled, they go.
'Neath Charlie's Wane they twitter and tweet,
And away they swarm 'neath the Dragon's feet,
With a whoop and a flutter they swing and sway,
And surge pell-mell down the Milky Way.
Between the legs of the glittering Chair
They hover and squeak in the empty air.
Then round they swoop past the glimmering Lion
To where Sirius barks behind huge Orion;
Up, then, and over to wheel amain
Under the silver, and home again.

—WALTER DE LA MARE

The New Suit

Striped suit,
a terrific tie,
buttoned shoes
and brown socks—
my outfit
for the party.

And the recommendations
drove me crazy—
—Don't eat ice cream
because it might drip.
—Juice, drink it slowly
since it dribbles.
—And nothing about
chocolate bombs
that might explode!
Happy birthday!
Who's that stuffed breathless
inside a tight suit?

Next year will be different.
I'll wear old clothes,
be ready to dribble,
and enjoy
ice cream, cake, and everything else.

—NIDIA SANABRIA DE ROMERO
Translated by Arnaldo D.
Larrosa Morán
with Naomi Shihab Nye

I met a King this afternoon!

I met a King this afternoon!
He had not on a Crown indeed,
A little Palmleaf Hat was all,
And he was barefoot, I'm afraid!

But sure I am he Ermine wore
Beneath his faded Jacket's blue—
And sure I am, the crest he bore
Within that Jacket's pocket too!

For 'twas too stately for an Earl—
A Marquis would not go so grand!
'Twas possibly a Czar petite—
A Pope, or something of that kind!

If I must tell you, of a Horse
My freckled Monarch held the rein—
Doubtless an estimable Beast,
But not at all disposed to run!

And such a wagon! While I live
Dare I presume to see
Another such a vehicle
As then transported me!

Two other ragged Princes
His royal state partook!
Doubtless the first excursion
These sovereigns ever took!

I question if the Royal Coach
Round which the Footmen wait
Has the significance, on high,
Of this Barefoot Estate!

—EMILY DICKINSON

There is no frigate like a book

There is no frigate like a book
    To take us lands away,
Nor any coursers like a page
    Of prancing poetry.
This traverse may the poorest take
    Without oppress of toll;
How frugal is the chariot
    That bears a human soul!

—EMILY DICKINSON

I'm nobody! Who are you?

I'm nobody! Who are you?
     Are you nobody, too?
Then there's a pair of us—don't tell!
They'd banish us, you know.

How dreary to be somebody!
How public, like a frog
To tell your name the livelong day
To an admiring bog!

—EMILY DICKINSON

"Hope" is the thing with feathers

"Hope" is the thing with feathers
  That perches in the soul,
  And sings the tune without the words,
  And never stops at all,

  And sweetest in the gale is heard;
  And sore must be the storm
  That could abash the little bird
  That kept so many warm.

  I've heard it in the chillest land,
  And on the strangest sea;
  Yet, never, in extremity,
  It asked a crumb of me.

—EMILY DICKINSON

A narrow Fellow in the Grass

A narrow Fellow in the Grass
Occasionally rides—
You may have met Him—did you not
His notice sudden is—

The Grass divides as with a Comb—
A spotted shaft is seen—
And then it closes at your feet
And opens further on—

He likes a Boggy Acre
A Floor too cool for Corn—
Yet when a Boy, and Barefoot—
I more than once at Noon

Have passed, I thought, a Whip lash
Unbraiding in the Sun
When stopping to secure it
It wrinkled, and was gone—

Several of Nature's People
I know, and they know me—
I feel for them a transport
Of cordiality—

But never met this Fellow
Attended, or alone
Without a tighter breathing
And Zero at the Bone—

—EMILY DICKINSON

[78]

The morns are meeker than they were

The morns are meeker than they were,
    The nuts are getting brown;
The berry's cheek is plumper,
    The rose is out of town.

The maple wears a gayer scarf,
    The field a scarlet gown.
Lest I should be old-fashioned,
    I'll put a trinket on.
        —EMILY DICKINSON

I never saw a moor

I never saw a moor,
I never saw the sea;
Yet know I how the heather looks,
And what a wave must be.

I never spoke with God,
Nor visited in heaven;
Yet certain am I of the spot
As if the chart were given.

—EMILY DICKINSON

A bird came down the walk

A bird came down the walk:
     He did not know I saw;
He bit an angle-worm in halves
And ate the fellow, raw.

And then he drank a dew
From a convenient grass,
And then hopped sidewise to the wall
To let a beetle pass.

He glanced with rapid eyes
That hurried all abroad,—
They looked like frightened beads, I thought;
He stirred his velvet head

Like one in danger; cautious,
I offered him a crumb,
And he unrolled his feathers
And rowed him softer home

Than oars divide the ocean,
Too silver for a seam,
Or butterflies, off banks of noon,
Leap, splashless, as they swim.

—EMILY DICKINSON

Freedom

Words, one by one
arrive on the empty page
like honored guests.
Ordered thoughts move
gracefully.
Outside the window,
on the sill,
I see the figure of a bird,
sun on its feathers—
a brownish, medium-sized bird.
I try to wave it away,
but it intrudes more stubbornly.
It has a quizzical look in its eye.
Ignoring its rude presence
I try to compose my lines,
but I feel uneasy
being observed by a brownish, medium-sized bird
with sun on its feathers—

—WIMAL DISSANAYAKE

Hold Fast Your Dreams

Hold fast your dreams!
Within your heart
Keep one, still, secret spot
Where dreams may go,
And sheltered so,
May thrive and grow—
Where doubt and fear are not.
O, keep a place apart,
Within your heart,
For little dreams to go!

Think still of lovely things that are not true.
Let wish and magic work at will in you.
Be sometimes blind to sorrow. Make believe!
Forget the calm that lies
In disillusioned eyes.
Though we all know that we must die,
Yet you and I
May walk like gods and be
Even now at home in immortality!

We see so many ugly things—
Deceits and wrongs and quarrelings;
We know, alas! we know
How quickly fade
The color in the west,
The bloom upon the flower,
The bloom upon the breast
And youth's blind hour.
Yet, keep within your heart
A place apart
Where little dreams may go,
May thrive and grow.
Hold fast—hold fast your dreams!

—LOUISE DRISCOLL

America

If an eagle be imprisoned
on the back of a coin,
and the coin be tossed
into the sky,
the coin will spin,
the coin will flutter,
but the eagle will never fly.

—HENRY DUMAS

Macavity: The Mystery Cat

Macavity's a Mystery Cat: he's called the Hidden Paw—
For he's the master criminal who can defy the Law.
He's the bafflement of Scotland Yard, the Flying Squad's despair:
For when they reach the scene of crime—*Macavity's not there!*

Macavity, Macavity, there's no one like Macavity,
He's broken every human law, he breaks the law of gravity.
His powers of levitation would make a fakir stare,
And when you reach the scene of crime—*Macavity's not there!*
You may seek him in the basement, you may look up in the air—
But I tell you once and once again, *Macavity's not there!*

Macavity's a ginger cat, he's very tall and thin;
You would know him if you saw him, for his eyes are sunken in.
His brow is deeply lined with thought, his head is highly domed;
His coat is dusty from neglect, his whiskers are uncombed.
He sways his head from side to side, with movements like a snake;
And when you think he's half asleep, he's always wide awake.

Macavity, Macavity, there's no one like Macavity,
For he's a fiend in feline shape, a monster of depravity.
You may meet him in a by-street, you may see him in the square—
But when a crime's discovered, then *Macavity's not there!*

He's outwardly respectable. (They say he cheats at cards.)
And his footprints are not found in any file of Scotland Yard's.
And when the larder's looted, or the jewel-case is rifled,
Or when the milk is missing, or another Peke's been stifled,
Or the greenhouse glass is broken, and the trellis past repair—
Ay, there's the wonder of the thing! *Macavity's not there!*

And when the Foreign Office find a Treaty's gone astray,
Or the Admiralty lose some plans and drawings by the way,
There may be a scrap of paper in the hall or on the stair—
But it's useless to investigate—*Macavity's not there!*
And when the loss has been disclosed, the Secret Service say:

"It *must* have been Macavity!"—but he's a mile away.
You'll be sure to find him resting, or a-licking of his thumbs,
Or engaged in doing complicated long division sums.

Macavity, Macavity, there's no one like Macavity,
There never was a Cat of such deceitfulness and suavity.
He always has an alibi, and one or two to spare:
At whatever time the deed took place—MACAVITY WASN'T
      THERE!
And they say that all the Cats whose wicked deeds are widely
      known
(I might mention Mungojerrie, I might mention Griddlebone)
Are nothing more than agents for the Cat who all the time
Just controls their operations: the Napoleon of Crime!

                             —T.S. ELIOT

Over the Garden Wall

Over the garden wall
Where unseen children play,
Somebody threw a ball
One fine summer day.
I caught it as it came
Straight from the hand unknown,
Playing a happy game
It would not play alone.

A pretty ball with bands
Of gold and stars of blue;
I turned it in my hands
And wondered, then I threw
Over the garden wall
Again the treasure round—
And somebody caught the ball
With a laughing sound.

—ELEANOR FARJEON

Wynken, Blynken, and Nod

Wynken, Blynken, and Nod one night
    Sailed off in a wooden shoe—
Sailed on a river of crystal light,
    Into a sea of dew.
"Where are you going, and what do you wish?"
    The old moon asked the three.
"We have come to fish for the herring fish
    That live in this beautiful sea;
    Nets of silver and gold have we,"
            Said Wynken,
            Blynken,
            And Nod.

The old moon laughed and sang a song,
    As they rocked in the wooden shoe,
And the wind that sped them all night long
    Ruffled the waves of dew.
The little stars were the herring fish
    That lived in that beautiful sea;
"Now cast your nets wherever you wish,
    Never afeared are we!"
So cried the stars to the fishermen three,
            Wynken,
            Blynken,
            And Nod.

All night long their nets they threw
    To the stars in the twinkling foam;
Then down from the sky came the wooden shoe,
    Bringing the fishermen home.
'Twas all so pretty a sail, it seemed
    As if it could not be;
And some folk thought 'twas a dream they'd dreamed
    Of sailing that beautiful sea;
But I shall name you the fishermen three,
            Wynken,
            Blynken,
            And Nod.

Wynken and Blynken are two little eyes,
  And Nod is a little head,
And the wooden shoe that sailed the skies
  Is a wee one's trundle bed.
So shut your eyes while Mother sings
  Of wonderful sights that be,
And you shall see the beautiful things
  As you rock in the misty sea
  Where the old shoe rocked the fishermen three,
        Wynken,
        Blynken,
        And Nod.

                              —EUGENE FIELD

Little Boy Blue

The little toy dog is covered with dust,
    But sturdy and staunch he stands;
And the little toy soldier is red with rust,
    And his musket moulds in his hands.
Time was when the little toy dog was new,
    And the soldier was passing fair;
And that was the time when our Little Boy Blue
    Kissed them and put them there.

"Now, don't you go till I come," he said,
    "And don't you make any noise!"
So, toddling off to his trundle-bed,
    He dreamt of the pretty toys;
And, as he was dreaming, an angel song
    Awakened our Little Boy Blue—
Oh! the years are many, the years are long,
    But the little toy friends are true!

Aye, faithful to Little Boy Blue they stand,
    Each in the same old place—
Awaiting the touch of a little hand,
    The smile of a little face;
And they wonder, as waiting the long years through
    In the dust of that little chair,
What has become of our Little Boy Blue,
    Since he kissed them and put them there.

—EUGENE FIELD

General Store

Some day I'm going to have a store
With a tinkly bell hung over the door,
With real glass cases and counters wide
And drawers all spilly with things inside.
There'll be a little of everything:
Bolts of calico; balls of string;
Jars of peppermint; tins of tea;
Pots and kettles and crockery;
Seeds in packets; scissors bright;
Kegs of sugar, brown and white;
Sarsaparilla for picnic lunches,
Bananas and rubber boots in bunches.
I'll fix the window and dust each shelf,
And take the money in all myself.
It will be my store, and I will say:
"What can I do for you today?"

—RACHEL FIELD

Skyscrapers

Do skyscrapers ever grow tired
Of holding themselves up high?
Do they ever shiver on frosty nights
With their tops against the sky?

Do they feel lonely sometimes
Because they have grown so tall?
Do they ever wish they could lie right down
And never get up at all?

—RACHEL FIELD

A Summer Morning

I saw dawn creep across the sky,
And all the gulls go flying by.
I saw the sea put on its dress
Of blue midsummer loveliness,
And heard the trees begin to stir
Green arms of pine and juniper.
I heard the wind call out and say,
"Get up, my dear, it is today!"

—RACHEL FIELD

Something Told the Wild Geese

Something told the wild geese
    It was time to go.
Though the fields lay golden
    Something whispered,—"Snow."
Leaves were green and stirring,
    Berries luster-glossed,
But beneath warm feathers
    Something cautioned,—"Frost."
All the sagging orchards
    Steamed with amber spice,
But each wild beast stiffened
    At remembered ice.
Something told the wild geese
    It was time to fly,—
Summer sun was on their wings,
    Winter in their cry.

—RACHEL FIELD

Some People

Isn't it strange some people make
    You feel so tired inside,
Your thoughts begin to shrivel up
    Like leaves all brown and dried!

But when you're with some other ones,
    It's stranger still to find
Your thoughts as thick as fireflies
    All shiny in your mind!

—RACHEL FIELD

Bouquets

One flower at a time, please
however small the face.

Two flowers are one flower
too many, a distraction.

Three flowers in a vase begin
to be a little noisy

Like cocktail conversation,
everybody talking.

A crowd of flowers is a crowd
of flatterers (forgive me).

One flower at a time. I want
to hear what it is saying.

— ROBERT FRANCIS

Mending Wall

Something there is that doesn't love a wall,
That sends the frozen-ground-swell under it,
And spills the upper boulders in the sun;
And makes gaps even two can pass abreast.
The work of hunters is another thing:
I have come after them and made repair
Where they have left not one stone on a stone,
But they would have the rabbit out of hiding,
To please the yelping dogs. The gaps I mean,
No one has seen them made or heard them made,
But at spring mending-time we find them there.
I let my neighbor know beyond the hill;
And on a day we meet to walk the line
And set the wall between us once again.
We keep the wall between us as we go.
To each the boulders that have fallen to each.
And some are loaves and some so nearly balls
We have to use a spell to make them balance:
"Stay where you are until our backs are turned!"
We wear our fingers rough with handling them.
Oh, just another kind of outdoor game,
One on a side. It comes to little more:
There where it is we do not need the wall:
He is all pine and I am apple orchard.
My apple trees will never get across
And eat the cones under his pines, I tell him.
He only says, "Good fences make good neighbors."
Spring is the mischief in me, and I wonder
If I could put a notion in his head:
"*Why* do they make good neighbors? Isn't it
Where there are cows? But here there are no cows.
Before I built a wall I'd ask to know
What I was walling in or walling out,
And to whom I was like to give offense.
Something there is that doesn't love a wall,
That wants it down." I could say "Elves" to him,
But it's not elves exactly, and I'd rather
He said it for himself. I see him there

Bringing a stone grasped firmly by the top
In each hand, like an old-stone savage armed.
He moves in darkness as it seems to me,
Not of woods only and the shade of trees.
He will not go behind his father's saying,
And he likes having thought of it so well
He says again, "Good fences make good neighbors."

—ROBERT FROST

Stopping by Woods on a Snowy Evening

Whose woods these are I think I know.
His house is in the village though;
He will not see me stopping here
To watch his woods fill up with snow.

My little horse must think it queer
To stop without a farmhouse near
Between the woods and frozen lake
The darkest evening of the year.

He gives his harness bells a shake
To ask if there is some mistake.
The only other sound's the sweep
Of easy wind and downy flake.

The woods are lovely, dark, and deep.
But I have promises to keep,
And miles to go before I sleep,
And miles to go before I sleep.

—ROBERT FROST

The Road Not Taken

Two roads diverged in a yellow wood,
And sorry I could not travel both
And be one traveler, long I stood
And looked down one as far as I could
To where it bent in the undergrowth;

Then took the other, as just as fair,
And having perhaps the better claim,
Because it was grassy and wanted wear;
Though as for that, the passing there
Had worn them really about the same,

And both that morning equally lay
In leaves no step had trodden black.
Oh, I kept the first for another day!
Yet knowing how way leads on to way,
I doubted if I should ever come back.

I shall be telling this with a sigh
Somewhere ages and ages hence:
Two roads diverged in a wood, and I—
I took the one less traveled by,
And that has made all the difference.

—ROBERT FROST

Dust of Snow

The way a crow
Shook down on me
The dust of snow
From a hemlock tree

Has given my heart
A change of mood
And saved some part
Of a day I had rued.

—ROBERT FROST

Mice

I think mice
Are rather nice.

Their tails are long,
Their faces small,
They haven't any
Chins at all.
Their ears are pink,
Their teeth are white,
They run about
The house at night
They nibble things
They shouldn't touch
And no one seems
To like them much.

But I think mice
Are nice.

—ROSE FYLEMAN

A Short Story

The ant climbs up a trunk
carrying a petal on its back;
and if you look closely
that petal is as big as a house
especially compared to the ant that
carries it so olympically.

You ask me: Why couldn't I carry
a petal twice as big as my body and my head?
Ah, but you can, little girl,
but not petals from a dahlia,
rather boxes full of thoughts
and loads of magic hours, and
a wagon of clear dreams, and
a big castle with its fairies:
all the petals that form the soul of
a little girl who speaks and speaks . . . !

—DAVID ESCOBAR GALINDO
Translated by Jorge D. Piche

Mr. Lizard Is Crying

For Mademoiselle Teresita Guillén
playing on a seven-note piano

Mr. lizard is crying.
Mrs. lizard is crying.

Mr. and Mrs. lizard
with little white bibs.

They have carelessly
lost their wedding ring.

Oh, their little ring of lead,
oh, their little leaden ring!

A big sky with nobody in it
rides the birds on its balloon.

The sun, that rounded captain,
wears a vest of satin.

See how old they are!
How old the lizards are!

Oh, how they cry and cry,
oh, oh, how they are crying!

—FEDERICO GARCÍA LORCA

Silly Song

Mama,
I wish I were silver.

Son,
You'd be very cold.

Mama,
I wish I were water.

Son,
You'd be very cold.

Mama,
Embroider me on your pillow.

That, yes!
Right away!

—FEDERICO GARCÍA LORCA

Plowing: A Memory

A lonely task it is to plow.
All day the black and shining soil
Rolls like a ribbon from the moldboard's
Glistening curve. All day the horses toil
And battle with the flies, and strain
Their creaking harnesses. All day
The crickets jeer from wind-blown shocks of grain.

October brings the frosty dawn,
The still warm noon, and cold, clear night
When stiffened crickets make no sound
And wild ducks in their southward flight
Go by in haste; and still the boy
And toiling team gnaw round after round
On weather-beaten stubble band by band,
Until at last, to his great joy,
The winter's frost seals up the unplowed land.

—HAMLIN GARLAND

I'd Love to Be a Fairy's Child

Children born of fairy stock
Never need for shirt or frock,
Never want for food or fire,
Always get their heart's desire:
Jingle pockets full of gold,
Marry when they're seven years old.
Every fairy child may keep
Two strong ponies and ten sheep;
All have houses, each his own,
Built of brick or granite stone;
They live on cherries, they run wild—
I'd love to be a Fairy's child.

—ROBERT GRAVES

The Dance

No one's dancing here tonight.
Wouldn't you know it.
The cat in profile smiles at the light,
the rain is just a little sound on the metal
of the roof—out of season.

The cat doesn't dance and I wouldn't watch
if she did. Her little soul though
dances tonight, she is so pleased we are alone.
She smells the roast in the kitchen
and for my sake appreciates its progress.

There is a little fire burning: sawdust pressed
into a log and sold for a dollar keeps the light
the right tone and the heat up, although
it isn't really cold. No one is dancing,
the candles have been punched out,

and the amber has worn off the hardwood box.
Even the music, if it were playing, would make it
no different. Not even the rain or the food.
It doesn't matter little friend.
No one's dancing here tonight—wouldn't you know it.

—DANIEL HALPERN

The Reminder

While I watch the Christmas blaze
Paint the room with ruddy rays,
Something makes my vision glide
To the frosty scene outside.

There, to reach a rotting berry,
Toils a thrush,—constrained to very
Dregs of food by sharp distress,
Taking such with thankfulness.

Why, O starving bird, when I
One day's joy would justify,
And put misery out of view,
Do you make me notice you!

—THOMAS HARDY

The Man He Killed

"Had he and I but met
By some old ancient inn,
We should have sat us down to wet
Right many a nipperkin!

"But ranged as infantry,
And staring face to face,
I shot at him as he at me,
And killed him in his place.

"I shot him dead because—
Because he was my foe,
Just so: my foe of course he was;
That's clear enough; although

"He thought he'd 'list, perhaps,
Off-hand like—just as I—
Was out of work—had sold his traps—
No other reason why.

"Yes; quaint and curious war is!
You shoot a fellow down
You'd treat if met where any bar is,
Or help to half-a-crown."

—THOMAS HARDY

The New Toy

She cannot leave it alone,
    The new toy;
She pats it, smooths it, rights it, to show it's her own,
As the other train-passengers muse on its temper and tone,
    Till she draws from it cries of annoy:—
She feigns to appear as if thinking it nothing so rare
    Or worthy of pride, to achieve
This wonder a child, though with reason the rest of them there
    May so be inclined to believe.

                          —THOMAS HARDY

The Oxen

Christmas Eve, and twelve of the clock.
    "Now they are all on their knees,"
An elder said as we sat in a flock
    By the embers in hearthside ease.

We pictured the meek mild creatures where
    They dwelt in their strawy pen,
Nor did it occur to one of us there
    To doubt they were kneeling then.

So fair a fancy few would weave
    In these years! Yet, I feel,
If someone said on Christmas Eve,
    "Come; see the oxen kneel

"In the lonely barton by yonder coomb
    Our childhood used to know,"
I should go with him in the gloom,
    Hoping it might be so.

—THOMAS HARDY

Those Winter Sundays

Sundays too my father got up early
and put his clothes on in the blueblack cold,
then with cracked hands that ached
from labor in the weekday weather made
banked fires blaze. No one ever thanked him.

I'd wake and hear the cold splintering, breaking.
When the rooms were warm, he'd call,
and slowly I would rise and dress,
fearing the chronic angers of that house,

Speaking indifferently to him,
who had driven out the cold
and polished my good shoes as well.
What did I know, what did I know
of love's austere and lonely offices?

         —ROBERT HAYDEN

Blackberry-Picking

For Philip Hobsbaum

Late August, given heavy rain and sun
For a full week, the blackberries would ripen.
At first, just one, a glossy purple clot
Among others, red, green, hard as a knot.
You ate that first one and its flesh was sweet
Like thickened wine: summer's blood was in it
Leaving stains upon the tongue and lust for
Picking. Then red ones inked up and that hunger
Sent us out with milk-cans, pea-tins, jam-pots
Where briars scratched and wet grass bleached our boots.
Round hayfields, cornfields and potato-drills
We trekked and picked until the cans were full,
Until the tinkling bottom had been covered
With green ones, and on top big dark blobs burned
Like a plate of eyes. Our hands were peppered
With thorn pricks, our palms sticky as Bluebeard's.

We hoarded the fresh berries in the byre.
But when the bath was filled we found a fur,
A rat-grey fungus, glutting on our cache.
The juice was stinking too. Once off the bush
The fruit fermented, the sweet flesh would turn sour.
I always felt like crying. It wasn't fair
That all the lovely canfuls smelt of rot.
Each year I hoped they'd keep, knew they would not.

—SEAMUS HEANEY

Scaffolding

Masons, when they start upon a building,
Are careful to test out the scaffolding;

Make sure that planks won't slip at busy points,
Secure all ladders, tighten bolted joints.

And yet all this comes down when the job's done
Showing off walls of sure and solid stone.

So if, my dear, there sometimes seem to be
Old bridges breaking between you and me

Never fear. We may let the scaffolds fall
Confident that we have built our wall.

—SEAMUS HEANEY

Napoleon

Children, when was
Napoleon Bonaparte
born? asks the teacher.

A thousand years ago, say the children.
A hundred years ago, say the children.
Nobody knows.

Children, what did
Napoleon Bonaparte
do? asks the teacher.

He won a war, say the children.
He lost a war, say the children.
Nobody knows.

Our butcher used to have a dog,
says Frankie,
and his name was Napoleon,
and the butcher used to beat him,
and the dog died
of hunger
a year ago.

And now all the children feel sorry
for Napoleon.

—MIROSLAV HOLUB
*Translated by Kaca
Polackova*

God's Grandeur

The world is charged with the grandeur of God.
    It will flame out, like shining from shook foil;
    It gathers to a greatness, like the ooze of oil
Crushed. Why do men then now not reck his rod?
Generations have trod, have trod, have trod;
    And all is seared with trade; bleared, smeared with toil;
    And wears man's smudge and shares man's smell: the soil
Is bare now, nor can foot feel, being shod.

And, for all this, nature is never spent;
    There lives the dearest freshness deep down things;
And though the last lights off the black West went
    Oh, morning, at the brown brink eastward, springs—
Because the Holy Ghost over the bent
    World broods with warm breast and with ah! bright wings.

—GERARD MANLEY HOPKINS

Pied Beauty

Glory be to God for dappled things—
    For skies of couple-colour as a brinded cow;
        For rose-moles all in stipple upon trout that swim;
Fresh-firecoal chestnut-falls; finches' wings;
    Landscape plotted and pieced—fold, fallow, and plough;
        And all trades, their gear and tackle and trim.
All things counter, original, spare, strange;
    Whatever is fickle, freckled (who knows how?)
        With swift, slow; sweet, sour; adazzle, dim;
He fathers-forth whose beauty is past change:
    Praise him.

—GERARD MANLEY HOPKINS

To an Athlete Dying Young

The time you won your town the race
We chaired you through the market-place;
Man and boy stood cheering by,
And home we brought you shoulder-high.

Today, the road all runners come,
Shoulder-high we bring you home,
And set you at your threshold down,
Townsman of a stiller town.

Smart lad, to slip betimes away
From fields where glory does not stay
And early though the laurel grows
It withers quicker than the rose.

Now you will not swell the rout
Of lads that wore their honors out,
Runners whom renown outran
And the name died before the man.

So set, before its echoes fade,
The fleet foot on the sill of shade,
And hold to the low lintel up
The still-defended challenge-cup.

And round that early-laureled head
Will flock to gaze the strengthless dead,
And find unwithered on its curls
The garland briefer than a girl's.

—A.E. HOUSMAN

When I Was One-and-Twenty

When I was one-and-twenty
    I heard a wise man say,
"Give crowns and pounds and guineas
    But not your heart away;
Give pearls away and rubies
    But keep your fancy free."
But I was one-and-twenty,
    No use to talk to me.

When I was one-and-twenty
    I heard him say again,
"The heart out of the bosom
    Was never given in vain;
'Tis paid with sighs a plenty
    And sold for endless rue."
And I am two-and-twenty,
    And oh, 'tis true, 'tis true.

—A.E. HOUSMAN

Loveliest of Trees, the Cherry Now

Loveliest of trees, the cherry now
Is hung with bloom along the bough,
And stands about the woodland ride
Wearing white for Eastertide.

Now, of my threescore years and ten,
Twenty will not come again,
And take from seventy springs a score,
It only leaves me fifty more.

And since to look at things in bloom
Fifty springs are little room,
About the woodlands I will go
To see the cherry hung with snow.

—A.E. HOUSMAN

The Sea Gypsy

I am fever'd with the sunset,
I am fretful with the bay,
For the wander-thirst is on me
And my soul is in Cathay.

There's a schooner in the offing,
With her topsails shot with fire,
And my heart has gone aboard her
For the Islands of Desire.

I must forth again to-morrow!
With the sunset I must be
Hull down on the trail of rapture
In the wonder of the Sea.

—RICHARD HOVEY

Miss Blues'es Child

If the blues would let me,
Lord knows I would smile.
If the blues would let me,
I would smile, smile, smile.
Instead of that I'm cryin'—
I must be Miss Blues'es child.

You were my moon up in the sky,
At night my wishing star.
I love you, oh, I love you so—
But you have gone so far!

Now my days are lonely,
And night-time drives me wild.
In my heart I'm crying,
I'm just Miss Blues'es child!

—LANGSTON HUGHES

Mother to Son

Well, son, I'll tell you,
Life for me ain't been no crystal stair.
It's had tacks in it,
And splinters,
And boards torn up,
And places with no carpet on the floor—
Bare.
But all the time
I'se been a-climbin' on,
And reachin' landin's,
And turnin' corners,
And sometimes goin' in the dark
Where there ain't been no light.
So, boy, don't you turn back.
Don't you set down on the steps
'Cause you finds it kinder hard.
Don't you fall now—
For I'se still goin', honey,
I'se still climbin',
And life for me ain't been no crystal stair.

—LANGSTON HUGHES

My Brother Bert

Pets are the hobby of my brother Bert.
He used to go to school with a mouse in his shirt.

His hobby it grew, as some hobbies will,
And grew and GREW and GREW until—

Oh don't breathe a word, pretend you haven't heard.
A simply appalling thing has occurred—

The very thought makes me iller and iller:
Bert's brought home a gigantic gorilla!

If you think that's really not such a scare,
What if it quarrels with his grizzly bear?

You still think you could keep your head?
What if the lion from under the bed

And the four ostriches that deposit
Their football eggs in his bedroom closet

And the aardvark out of his bottom drawer
All danced out and joined in the roar?

What if the pangolins were to caper
Out of their nests behind the wallpaper?

With the fifty sorts of bats
That hang on his hatstand like old hats,

And out of a shoebox the excitable platypus
Along with the ocelot or jungle-cattypus?

The wombat, the dingo, the gecko, the grampus—
How they would shake the house with their rumpus!

Not to forget the bandicoot
Who would certainly peer from his battered old boot.

Why it could be a dreadful day,
And what, oh what, would the neighbors say!

—TED HUGHES

Roger the Dog

Asleep he wheezes at his ease.
He only wakes to scratch his fleas.

He hogs the fire, he bakes his head
As if it were a loaf of bread.

He's just a sack of snoring dog.
You can lug him like a log.

You can roll him with your foot,
He'll stay snoring where he's put.

I take him out for exercise,
He rolls in cowclap up to his eyes.

He will not race, he will not romp,
He saves his strength for gobble and chomp.

He'll work as hard as you could wish
Emptying his dinner dish,

Then flops flat, and digs down deep,
Like a miner, into sleep.

—TED HUGHES

Abou Ben Adhem

Abou Ben Adhem (may his tribe increase!)
Awoke one night from a deep dream of peace,
And saw, within the moonlight in his room,
Making it rich, and like a lily in bloom,
An Angel writing in a book of gold:
Exceeding peace had made Ben Adhem bold,
And to the Presence in the room he said,
"What writest thou?" The Vision raised its head,
And with a look made of all sweet accord
Answered, "The names of those who love the Lord."
"And is mine one?" said Abou. "Nay, not so,"
Replied the Angel. Abou spoke more low,
But cheerily still; and said, "I pray thee, then,
Write me as one that loves his fellow men."

The Angel wrote, and vanished. The next night
It came again with a great wakening light,
And showed the names whom love of God had blessed,
And, lo! Ben Adhem's name led all the rest!

—JAMES HENRY LEIGH HUNT

Don't worry, spiders,
I keep house
      casually.

—KOBAYASHI ISSA

Don't kill that fly!
Look—it's wringing its hands,
      wringing its feet.

—KOBAYASHI ISSA

Under the evening moon
the snail
      is stripped to the waist.

—KOBAYASHI ISSA

For you fleas too
the nights must be long,
they must be lonely.
—KOBAYASHI ISSA

Even with insects—
some can sing,
some can't.
—KOBAYASHI ISSA

Climb Mount Fuji,
O snail,
But slowly, slowly.
—KOBAYASHI ISSA

Mosquito at my ear—
does it think
I'm deaf?

—KOBAYASHI ISSA

Bats

A bat is born
Naked and blind and pale.
His mother makes a pocket of her tail
And catches him. He clings to her long fur
By his thumbs and toes and teeth.
And then the mother dances through the night
Doubling and looping, soaring, somersaulting—
Her baby hangs on underneath.
All night, in happiness, she hunts and flies.
Her high sharp cries
Like shining needlepoints of sound
Go out into the night and, echoing back,
Tell her what they have touched.
She hears how far it is, how big it is,
Which way it's going:
She lives by hearing.
The mother eats the moths and gnats she catches
In full flight; in full flight
The mother drinks the water of the pond
She skims across. Her baby hangs on tight.
Her baby drinks the milk she makes him
In moonlight or starlight, in mid-air.
Their single shadow, printed on the moon
Or fluttering across the stars,
Whirls on all night; at daybreak
The tired mother flaps home to her rafter.
The others all are there.
They hang themselves up by their toes,
They wrap themselves in their brown wings.
Bunched upside-down, they sleep in air.
Their sharp ears, their sharp teeth, their quick sharp faces
Are dull and slow and mild.
All the bright day, as the mother sleeps,
She folds her wings about her sleeping child.

—RANDALL JARRELL

Autumn Evening

Though the little clouds ran southward still, the quiet autumnal
Cool of the late September evening
Seemed promising rain, rain, the change of the year, the angel
Of the sad forest. A heron flew over
With that remote ridiculous cry, "Quawk," the cry
That seems to make silence more silent. A dozen
Flops of the wing, a drooping glide, at the end of the glide
The cry, and a dozen flops of the wing.
I watched him pass on the autumn-colored sky; beyond him
Jupiter shone for evening star.
The sea's voice worked into my mood, I thought "No matter
What happens to men . . . the world's well made though."

—ROBINSON JEFFERS

Hurt Hawks

1

The broken pillar of the wing jags from the clotted shoulder,
The wing trails like a banner in defeat,
No more to use the sky forever but live with famine
And pain a few days: cat nor coyote
Will shorten the week of waiting for death, there is game without
    talons.
He stands under the oak-bush and waits
The lame feet of salvation; at night he remembers freedom
And flies in a dream, the dawns ruin it.
He is strong and pain is worse to the strong, incapacity is worse.
The curs of the day come and torment him
At distance, no one but death the redeemer will humble that head,
The intrepid readiness, the terrible eyes.
The wild God of the world is sometimes merciful to those
That ask mercy, not often to the arrogant.
You do not know him, you communal people, or you have
    forgotten him;
Intemperate and savage, the hawk remembers him;
Beautiful and wild, the hawks, and men that are dying, remember
    him.

2

I'd sooner, except the penalties, kill a man than a hawk; but the
    great redtail
Had nothing left but unable misery
From the bone too shattered for mending, the wing that trailed
    under his talons when he moved.
We had fed him six weeks, I gave him freedom,
He wandered over the foreland hill and returned in the evening,
    asking for death,
Not like a beggar, still eyed with the old
Implacable arrogance. I gave him the lead gift in the twilight.
    What fell was relaxed,
Owl-downy, soft feminine feathers; but what

Soared: the fierce rush: the night-herons by the flooded river cried
     fear at its rising
Before it was quite unsheathed from reality.

—ROBINSON JEFFERS

Minnows

. . . Swarms of minnows show their little heads,
Staying their waxy bodies 'gainst the streams,
To taste the luxury of sunny beams
Tempered with coolness. How they ever wrestle
With their own sweet delight, and ever nestle
Their silver bellies on the pebbly sand.
If you but scantily hold out the hand,
That very instant not one will remain;
But turn your eye, and they are there again.
The ripples seem right glad to reach those cresses,
And cool themselves among the em'rald tresses;
The while they cool themselves, they freshness give,
And moisture, that the bowery green may live.

—JOHN KEATS

Ode on a Grecian Urn

1

Thou still unravish'd bride of quietness,
    Thou foster-child of silence and slow time,
Sylvan historian, who canst thus express
    A flowery tale more sweetly than our rhyme:
What leaf-fring'd legend haunts about thy shape
    Of deities or mortals, or of both,
        In Tempe or the dales of Arcady?
    What men or gods are these? What maidens loth?
What mad pursuit? What struggle to escape?
    What pipes and timbrels? What wild ecstasy?

2

Heard melodies are sweet, but those unheard
    Are sweeter; therefore, ye soft pipes, play on;
Not to the sensual ear, but, more endear'd,
    Pipe to the spirit ditties of no tone:
Fair youth, beneath the trees, thou canst not leave
    Thy song, nor ever can those trees be bare;
        Bold lover, never, never canst thou kiss,
Though winning near the goal—yet, do not grieve;
    She cannot fade, though thou hast not thy bliss,
For ever wilt thou love, and she be fair!

3

Ah, happy, happy boughs! that cannot shed
    Your leaves, nor ever bid the spring adieu;
And, happy melodist, unwearied,
    For ever piping songs for ever new;
More happy love! more happy, happy love!
    For ever warm and still to be enjoy'd,
        For ever panting, and for ever young;
All breathing human passion far above,
    That leaves a heart high-sorrowful and cloy'd,
        A burning forehead, and a parching tongue.

4

Who are these coming to the sacrifice?
 To what green altar, O mysterious priest,
Lead'st thou that heifer lowing at the skies,
 And all her silken flanks with garlands drest?
What little town by river or sea shore,
 Or mountain-built with peaceful citadel,
 Is emptied of this folk, this pious morn?
And, little town, thy streets for evermore
 Will silent be; and not a soul to tell
 Why thou art desolate, can e'er return.

5

O Attic shape! Fair attitude! with brede
 Of marble men and maidens overwrought,
With forest branches and the trodden weed;
 Thou, silent form, dost tease us out of thought
As doth eternity: Cold Pastoral!
 When old age shall this generation waste,
 Thou shalt remain, in midst of other woe
 Than ours, a friend to man, to whom thou say'st,
"Beauty is truth, truth beauty,"—that is all
 Ye know on earth, and all ye need to know.

—JOHN KEATS

Mother's Nerves

My mother said, "If just once more
I hear you slam that old screen door,
I'll tear out my hair! I'll dive in the stove!"
I gave it a bang and in she dove.

—X.J. KENNEDY

Trees

I think that I shall never see
A poem lovely as a tree.

A tree whose hungry mouth is pressed
Against the earth's sweet flowing breast;

A tree that looks at God all day
And lifts her leafy arms to pray;

A tree that may in summer wear
A nest of robins in her hair;

Upon whose bosom snow has lain;
Who intimately lives with rain.

Poems are made by fools like me,
But only God can make a tree.

—JOYCE KILMER

The House with Nobody in It

Whenever I walk to Suffern along the Erie track,
I go by a poor old farmhouse with its shingles broken and black.
I suppose I've passed it a hundred times, but I always stop for a
    minute,
And look at the house, the tragic house, the house with nobody
    in it.

I never have seen a haunted house, but I hear there are such things;
That they hold the talk of spirits, their mirth and sorrowings.
I know this house isn't haunted, and I wish it were, I do;
For it wouldn't be so lonely if it had a ghost or two.

This house on the road to Suffern needs a dozen panes of glass,
And somebody ought to weed the walk and take a scythe to the
    grass.
It needs new paint and shingles, and the vines should be trimmed
    and tied;
But what it needs the most of all is some people living inside.

If I had a lot of money and all my debts were paid,
I'd put a gang of men to work with brush and saw and spade.
I'd buy that place and fix it up the way it used to be
And I'd find some people who wanted a home and give it to them
    free.

Now, a new house standing empty, with staring window and door,
Looks idle, perhaps, and foolish, like a hat on its block in the
    store.
But there's nothing mournful about it; it can not be sad and lone
For the lack of something within it that it has never known.

But a house that has done what a house should do, a house that
    has sheltered life,
That has put its loving wooden arms around a man and his wife,
A house that has echoed a baby's laugh and held up his stumbling
    feet,
Is the saddest sight, when it's left alone, that ever your eyes could
    meet.

So whenever I go to Suffern along the Erie track,
I never go by the empty house without stopping and looking back,
Yet it hurts me to look at the crumbling roof and the shutters
   fallen apart,
For I can't help thinking the poor old house is a house with a
   broken heart.

— JOYCE KILMER

Crying

Crying only a little bit
is no use. You must cry
until your pillow is soaked!
Then you can get up and laugh.
Then you can jump in the shower
and splash-splash-splash!
Then you can throw open your window
and, "Ha ha! ha ha!"
And if people say, "Hey,
what's going on up there?"
"Ha ha!" sing back, "Happiness
was hiding in the last tear!
I wept it! Ha ha!"

—GALWAY KINNELL

Saint Francis and the Sow

The bud
stands for all things,
even for those things that don't flower,
for everything flowers, from within, of self-blessing;
though sometimes it is necessary
to reteach a thing its loveliness,
to put a hand on its brow
of the flower
and retell it in words and in touch
it is lovely
until it flowers again from within, of self-blessing;
as Saint Francis
put his hand on the creased forehead
of the sow, and told her in words and in touch
blessings of earth on the sow, and the sow
began remembering all down her thick length,
from the earthen snout all the way
through the fodder and slops to the spiritual curl of the tail,
from the hard spininess spiked out from the spine
down through the great broken heart
to the sheer blue milken dreaminess spurting and shuddering
from the fourteen teats into the fourteen mouths sucking and
       blowing beneath them:
the long, perfect loveliness of sow.

—GALWAY KINNELL

Daybreak

On the tidal mud, just before sunset,
dozens of starfishes
were creeping. It was as though the mud were a sky
and enormous, imperfect stars
moved across it as slowly
as the actual stars cross heaven.
All at once they stopped,
and as if they had simply
increased their receptivity
to gravity they sank down
into the mud; they faded down
into it and lay still; and by the time
pink of sunset broke across them
they were as invisible
as the true stars at daybreak.

—GALWAY KINNELL

The Way through the Woods

They shut the road through the woods
    Seventy years ago.
Weather and rain have undone it again,
    And now you would never know
There was once a path through the woods
    Before they planted the trees.
It is underneath the coppice and heath,
    And the thin anemonies.
    Only the keeper sees
That, where the ringdove broods,
    And the badgers roll at ease,
There was once a road through the woods.
Yet, if you enter the woods
    Of a summer evening late,
When the night air cools on the trout-ring'd pools
    Where the otter whistles his mate
(They fear not men in the woods
    Because they see so few),
You will hear the beat of a horse's feet
    And the swish of a skirt in the dew,
    Steadily cantering through
The misty solitudes,
    As though they perfectly knew
The old lost road through the woods . . .
But there is no road through the woods.

—RUDYARD KIPLING

If—

If you can keep your head when all about you
     Are losing theirs and blaming it on you;
If you can trust yourself when all men doubt you,
     But make allowance for their doubting too;
If you can wait and not be tired by waiting,
     Or, being lied about, don't deal in lies,
Or, being hated, don't give way to hating,
     And yet don't look too good, nor talk too wise;

If you can dream—and not make dreams your master;
     If you can think—and not make thoughts your aim;
If you can meet with triumph and disaster
     And treat those two imposters just the same;
If you can bear to hear the truth you've spoken
     Twisted by knaves to make a trap for fools,
Or watch the things you gave your life to broken,
     And stoop and build 'em up with wornout tools;

If you can make one heap of all your winnings
     And risk it on one turn of pitch-and-toss,
And lose, and start again at your beginnings
     And never breathe a word about your loss;
If you can force your heart and nerve and sinew
     To serve your turn long after they are gone,
And so hold on when there is nothing in you
     Except the Will which says to them: "Hold on";

If you can talk with crowds and keep your virtue,
     Or walk with kings—nor lose the common touch;
If neither foes nor loving friends can hurt you;
     If all men count with you, but none too much;
If you can fill the unforgiving minute
     With sixty seconds' worth of distance run—
Yours is the Earth and everything that's in it,
     And—which is more—you'll be a Man, my son!

—RUDYARD KIPLING

The Idea of Ancestry

1

Taped to the wall of my cell are 47 pictures: 47 black
faces: my father, mother, grandmothers (1 dead), grand-
fathers (both dead), brothers, sisters, uncles, aunts,
cousins (1st & 2nd), nieces, and nephews. They stare
across the space at me sprawling on my bunk. I know
their dark eyes, they know mine. I know their style,
they know mine. I am all of them, they are all of me;
they are farmers, I am a thief, I am me, they are thee.

I have at one time or another been in love with my mother,
1 grandmother, 2 sisters, 2 aunts (1 went to the asylum),
and 5 cousins. I am now in love with a 7 yr old niece
(she sends me letters written in large block print, and
her picture is the only one that smiles at me).

I have the same name as 1 grandfather, 3 cousins, 3 nephews,
and 1 uncle. The uncle disappeared when he was 15, just took
off and caught a freight (they say). He's discussed each year
when the family has a reunion, he causes uneasiness in
the clan, he is an empty space. My father's mother, who is 93
and who keeps the Family Bible with everybody's birth dates
(and death dates) in it, always mentions him. There is no
place in her Bible for "whereabouts unknown."

2

Each fall the graves of my grandfathers call me, the brown
hills and red gullies of Mississippi send out their electric
messages, galvanizing my genes. Last yr / like a salmon quitting
the cold ocean-leaping and bucking up his birthstream / I
hitchhiked my way from L.A. with 16 caps in my pocket and a
monkey on my back. And I almost kicked it with the kinfolks.
I walked barefooted in my grandmother's backyard / I smelled the
　　　old
land and the woods / I sipped cornwhiskey from fruit jars with the
　　　men /

[148]

I flirted with the women / I had a ball till the caps ran out
and my habit came down. That night I looked at my grandmother
and split / my guts were screaming for junk / but I was almost
contented / I had almost caught up with me,
(The next day in Memphis I cracked a croaker's crib for a fix.)

This yr there is a gray stone wall damming my stream, and when
the falling leaves stir my genes, I pace my cell or flop on my bunk
and stare at 47 black faces across the space. I am all of them,
they are all of me, I am me, they are thee, and I have no children
to float in the space between.

—ETHERIDGE KNIGHT

Snake

A snake came to my water-trough
On a hot, hot day, and I in pajamas for the heat,
To drink there.

In the deep, strange-scented shade of the great dark carob-tree
I came down the steps with my pitcher
And must wait, must stand and wait, for there he was at the
      trough before me.

He reached down from the fissure in the earth-wall in the gloom
And trailed his yellow-brown slackness soft-bellied down, over the
      edge of the stone trough
And rested his throat upon the stone bottom,
And where the water had dripped from the tap, in a small
      clearness,
He sipped with his straight mouth,
Softly drank through his straight gums, into his slack long body,
Silently.

Someone was before me at my water-trough,
And I, like a second comer, waiting.

He lifted his head from his drinking, as cattle do,
And looked at me vaguely, as drinking cattle do,
And flickered his two-forked tongue from his lips, and mused a
      moment,
And stooped and drank a little more,
Being earth-brown, earth-golden from the burning bowels of the
      earth
On the day of Sicilian July, with Etna smoking.

The voice of my education said to me
He must be killed,
For in Sicily the black, black snakes are innocent, the gold are
      venomous.

And voices in me said, If you were a man
You would take a stick and break him now, and finish him off.

But must I confess how I liked him,
How glad I was he had come like a guest in quiet, to drink at my
      water-trough
And depart peaceful, pacified, and thankless,
Into the burning bowels of this earth?

Was it cowardice, that I dared not kill him?
Was it perversity, that I longed to talk to him?
Was it humility, to feel so honoured?
I felt so honoured.

And yet those voices:
If you were not afraid, you would kill him!

And truly I was afraid, I was most afraid,
But even so, honoured still more
That he should seek my hospitality
From out the dark door of the secret earth.

He drank enough
And lifted his head, dreamily, as one who has drunken,
And flickered his tongue like a forked night on the air, so black,
Seeming to lick his lips,
And looked around like a god, unseeing, into the air,
And slowly turned his head,
And slowly, very slowly, as if thrice adream,
Proceeded to draw his slow length curving round
And climb again the broken bank of my wall-face.

And as he put his head into that dreadful hole,
And as he slowly drew up, snake-easing his shoulders, and entered
      farther,
A sort of horror, a sort of protest against his withdrawing into that
      horrid black hole,
Deliberately going into the blackness, and slowly drawing himself
      after,
Overcame me now his back was turned.

[151]

I looked round, I put down my pitcher,
I picked up a clumsy log
And threw it at the water-trough with a clatter.

I think it did not hit him,
But suddenly that part of him that was left behind convulsed in
        undignified haste,
Writhed like lightening, and was gone
Into the black hole, the earth-lipped fissure in the wall-front,
At which, in the intense still noon, I stared with fascination.

And immediately I regretted it.
I thought how paltry, how vulgar, what a mean act!
I despised myself and the voices of my accursed human education.
And I thought of the albatross,
And I wished he would come back, my snake.

For he seemed to me again like a king,
Like a king in exile, uncrowned in the underworld,
Now due to be crowned again.

And so, I missed my chance with one of the lords
Of life.
And I have something to expiate;
A pettiness.

—D.H. LAWRENCE

The Owl and the Pussycat

The Owl and the Pussycat went to sea
    In a beautiful pea-green boat:
They took some honey, and plenty of money
    Wrapped up in a five-pound note.
The Owl looked up to the stars above,
    And sang to a small guitar,
"O lovely Pussy, O Pussy, my love,
    What a beautiful Pussy you are,
        You are,
        You are!
What a beautiful Pussy you are!"

Pussy said to the Owl, "You elegant fowl,
    How charmingly sweet you sing!
Oh! let us be married; too long we have tarried:
    But what shall we do for a ring?"
They sailed away, for a year and a day,
    To the land where the bong tree grows;
And there in a wood a Piggy-wig stood,
    With a ring at the end of his nose,
        His nose,
        His nose,
With a ring at the end of his nose.

"Dear Pig, are you willing to sell for one shilling
    Your ring?" Said the Piggy, "I will."
So they took it away, and were married next day
    By the Turkey who lives on the hill.
They dined on mince and slices of quince,
    Which they ate with a runcible spoon;
And hand in hand, on the edge of the sand,
    They danced by the light of the moon,
        The moon,
        The moon,
They danced by the light of the moon.

              — EDWARD LEAR

Viewing the Waterfall at Mount Lu

Sunlight streaming on Incense Stone kindles violet
    smoke;
far off I watch the waterfall plunge to the long river,
flying waters descending straight three thousand feet,
till I think the Milky Way has tumbled from the
    ninth height of Heaven.

—LI PO

The Children's Hour

Between the dark and the daylight,
          When the night is beginning to lower,
Comes a pause in the day's occupations,
          That is known as the Children's Hour.

I hear in the chamber above me
          The patter of little feet,
The sound of a door that is opened,
          And voices soft and sweet.

From my study I see in the lamplight,
          Descending the broad hall stair,
Grave Alice, and laughing Allegra,
          And Edith with golden hair.

A whisper, and then a silence:
          Yet I know by their merry eyes
They are plotting and planning together
          To take me by surprise.

A sudden rush from the stairway,
          A sudden raid from the hall!
By three doors left unguarded
          They enter my castle wall!

They climb up into my turret
          O'er the arms and back of my chair;
If I try to escape, they surround me;
          They seem to be everywhere.

They almost devour me with kisses,
          Their arms about me entwine,
Till I think of the Bishop of Bingen
          In his Mouse-Tower on the Rhine!

Do you think, O blue-eyed banditti,
        Because you have scaled the wall,
Such an old mustache as I am
        Is not a match for you all!

I have you fast in my fortress,
        And will not let you depart,
But put you down into the dungeon
        In the round-tower of my heart.

And there will I keep you forever,
        Yes, forever and a day,
Till the walls shall crumble to ruin,
        And moulder in dust away!

—HENRY WADSWORTH LONGFELLOW

The Day Is Done

The day is done, and the darkness
    Falls from the wings of Night,
As a feather is wafted downward
    From an eagle in his flight.

I see the lights of the village
    Gleam through the rain and the mist,
And a feeling of sadness comes o'er me
    That my soul cannot resist:

A feeling of sadness and longing,
    That is not akin to pain,
And resembles sorrow only
    As the mist resembles the rain.

Come, read to me some poem,
    Some simple and heartfelt lay,
That shall soothe this restless feeling,
    And banish the thoughts of day.

Not from the grand old masters,
    Not from the bards sublime,
Whose distant footsteps echo
    Through the corridors of time.

For, like strains of martial music,
    Their mighty thoughts suggest
Life's endless toil and endeavor;
    And to-night I long for rest.

Read from some humbler poet,
    Whose songs gushed from his heart,
As showers from the clouds of summer,
    Or tears from the eyelids start;

Who, through long days of labor,
    And nights devoid of ease,
Still heard in his soul the music
    Of wonderful melodies.

Such songs have power to quiet
    The restless pulse of care,
And come like the benediction
    That follows after prayer.

Then read from the treasured volume
    The poem of thy choice,
And lend to the rhyme of the poet
    The beauty of thy voice.

And the night shall be filled with music,
    And the cares, that infest the day,
Shall fold their tents, like the Arabs,
    And as silently steal away.

            —HENRY WADSWORTH LONGFELLOW

The Village Blacksmith

Under a spreading chestnut tree
    The village smithy stands;
The smith, a mighty man is he,
    With large and sinewy hands;
And the muscles of his brawny arms
    Are strong as iron bands.

His hair is crisp, and black, and long,
    His face is like the tan;
His brow is wet with honest sweat,
    He earns whate'er he can,
And looks the whole world in the face,
    For he owes not any man.

Week in, week out, from morn till night,
    You can hear his bellows blow;
You can hear him swing his heavy sledge,
    With measured beat and slow,
Like a sexton ringing the village bell,
    When the evening sun is low.
And children coming home from school
    Look in at the open door;
They love to see the flaming forge,
    And hear the bellows roar,
And catch the burning sparks that fly
    Like chaff from a threshing floor.

He goes on Sunday to the church,
    And sits among his boys;
He hears the parson pray and preach,
    He hears his daughter's voice,
Singing in the village choir,
    And it makes his heart rejoice.

It sounds to him like her mother's voice,
    Singing in Paradise.
He needs must think of her once more,
    How in the grave she lies;

And with his hard, rough hand he wipes
A tear out of his eyes.

Toiling, rejoicing, sorrowing,
Onward through life he goes;
Each morning sees some task begun,
Each evening sees it close;
Something attempted, something done,
Has earned a night's repose.

—HENRY WADSWORTH LONGFELLOW

Paul Revere's Ride

Listen, my children, and you shall hear
Of the midnight ride of Paul Revere,
On the eighteenth of April, in Seventy-five;
Hardly a man is now alive
Who remembers that famous day and year.

He said to his friend, "If the British march
By land or sea from the town tonight,
Hang a lantern aloft in the belfry arch
Of the North Church tower as a signal light—
One, if by land, and two, if by sea;
And I on the opposite shore will be,
Ready to ride and spread the alarm
Through every Middlesex village and farm,
For the country folk to be up and to arm."

Then he said, "Good night!" and with muffled oar
Silently rowed to the Charlestown shore,
Just as the moon rose over the bay,
Where swinging wide at her moorings lay
The *Somerset*, British man-of-war;
A phantom ship, with each mast and spar
Across the moon like a prison bar,
And a huge black hulk, that was magnified
By its own reflection in the tide.

Meanwhile, his friend, through alley and street,
Wanders and watches, with eager ears,
Till in the silence around him he hears
The muster of men at the barrack door,
And the measured tread of the grenadiers,
Marching down to their boats on the shore.

Then he climbed to the tower of the Old North Church,
By the wooden stairs, with stealthy tread,
To the belfry-chamber overhead,
And startled the pigeons from their perch
On the somber rafters, that round him made

Masses and moving shapes of shade—
By the trembling ladder, steep and tall,
To the highest window in the wall,
Where he paused to listen and look down
A moment on the roofs of the town,
And the moonlight flowing over all.

Beneath in the churchyard, lay the dead,
In their night-encampment on the hill,
Wrapped in silence so deep and still
That he could hear, like a sentinel's tread,
The watchful night-wind, as it went
Creeping along from tent to tent,
And seeming to whisper, "All is well!"
A moment only he feels the spell
Of the place and the hour, and the secret dread
Of the lonely belfry and the dead;
For suddenly all his thoughts are bent
On a shadowy something far away,
Where the river widens to meet the bay—
A line of black that bends and floats
On the rising tide, like a bridge of boats.

Meanwhile, impatient to mount and ride,
Booted and spurred, with a heavy stride
On the opposite shore walked Paul Revere.
Now he patted his horse's side,
Now gazed at the landscape far and near,
Then, impetuous, stamped the earth,
And turned and tightened his saddle girth;
But mostly he watched with eager search
The belfry tower of the Old North Church,
As it rose above the graves on the hill,
Lonely and spectral and somber and still.

And lo! as he looks, on the belfry's height
A glimmer, and then a gleam of light!
He springs to the saddle, the bridle he turns,

But lingers and gazes, till full on his sight
A second lamp in the belfry burns!

A hurry of hoofs in a village street,
A shape in the moonlight, a bulk in the dark,
And beneath, from the pebbles, in passing, a spark
Struck out by a steed flying fearless and fleet:
That was all! And yet, through the gloom and the light,
The fate of a nation was riding that night;
And the spark struck out by that steed, in his flight,
Kindled the land into flame with its heat.

He has left the village and mounted the steep,
And beneath him, tranquil and broad and deep,
Is the Mystic, meeting the ocean tides;
And under the alders that skirt its edge,
Now soft on the sand, now loud on the ledge,
Is heard the tramp of his steed as he rides.

It was twelve by the village clock,
When he crossed the bridge into Medford town.
He heard the crowing of the cock,
And the barking of the farmer's dog,
And felt the damp of the river fog,
That rises after the sun goes down.
It was one by the village clock,
When he galloped into Lexington.
He saw the gilded weathercock
Swim in the moonlight as he passed,
And the meeting-house windows, blank and bare,
Gaze at him with a spectral glare,
As if they already stood aghast
At the bloody work they would look upon.

It was two by the village clock,
When he came to the bridge in Concord town.
He heard the bleating of the flock,
And the twitter of birds among the trees,

And felt the breath of the morning breeze
Blowing over the meadows brown.
And one was safe and asleep in his bed
Who at the bridge would be first to fall,
Who that day would be lying dead,
Pierced by a British musket-ball.

You know the rest. In the books you have read
How the British Regulars fired and fled—
How the farmers gave them ball for ball,
From behind each fence and farmyard wall,
Chasing the red-coats down the lane,
Then crossing the fields to emerge again
Under the trees at the turn of the road,
And only pausing to fire and load.

So through the night rode Paul Revere;
And so through the night went his cry of alarm
To every Middlesex village and farm—
A cry of defiance and not of fear,
A voice in the darkness, a knock at the door,
And a word that shall echo for evermore!
For, borne on the night-wind of the Past,
Through all our history, to the last,
In the hour of darkness and peril and need,
The people will awaken and listen to hear
The hurrying hoof-beats of that steed,
And the midnight message of Paul Revere.

—HENRY WADSWORTH LONGFELLOW

Sea Fever

I must go down to the seas again, to the lonely sea and the sky,
And all I ask is a tall ship and a star to steer her by,
And the wheel's kick and the wind's song and the white sail's
      shaking,
And a gray mist on the sea's face, and a gray dawn breaking.

I must go down to the seas again, for the call of the running tide
Is a wild call and a clear call that may not be denied;
And all I ask is a windy day with the white clouds flying,
And the flung spray and the blown spume, and the sea gulls
      crying.

I must go down to the seas again, to the vagrant gypsy life,
To the gull's way and the whale's way where the wind's like a
      whetted knife;
And all I ask is a merry yarn from a laughing fellow-rover,
And quiet sleep and a sweet dream when the long trick's over.

                                  —JOHN MASEFIELD

In Flanders Fields

In Flanders Fields the poppies blow
Between the crosses, row on row,
That mark our place; and in the sky
The larks, still bravely singing, fly
Scarce heard amid the guns below.

We are the dead. Short days ago
We lived, felt dawn, saw sunset glow,
Loved and were loved, and now we lie
    In Flanders Fields.

Take up our quarrel with the foe;
To you from failing hands we throw
The torch; be yours to hold it high.
If ye break faith with us who die
We shall not sleep, though poppies grow
    In Flanders Fields.

—JOHN MCCRAE

Spring in New Hampshire

To J. L. J. F. E

Too green the springing April grass,
    Too blue the silver-speckled sky,
For me to linger here, alas,
    While happy winds go laughing by,
Wasting the golden hours indoors,
Washing windows and scrubbing floors.

Too wonderful the April night,
    Too faintly sweet the first May flowers,
The stars too gloriously bright,
    For me to spend the evening hours,
When fields are fresh and streams are leaping,
Wearied, exhausted, dully sleeping.

—CLAUDE MCKAY

The Pirate Don Durk of Dowdee

Ho, for the Pirate Don Durk of Dowdee!
He was as wicked as wicked could be,
But oh, he was perfectly gorgeous to see!
    The Pirate Don Durk of Dowdee.

His conscience, of course, was as black as a bat,
But he had a floppety plume on his hat
And when he went walking it jiggled—like that!
    The plume of the Pirate Dowdee.

His coat it was crimson and cut with a slash,
And often as ever he twirled his mustache.
Deep down in the ocean the mermaids went splash,
    Because of Don Durk of Dowdee.

Moreover, Dowdee had a purple tattoo,
And stuck in his belt where he buckled it through
Were a dagger, a dirk and a squizzamaroo,
    For fierce was the Pirate Dowdee.

So fearful he was he would shoot at a puff,
And always at sea when the weather grew rough
He drank from a bottle and wrote on his cuff,
    Did Pirate Don Durk of Dowdee.

Oh, he had a cutlass that swung at his thigh
And he had a parrot called Pepperkin Pye,
And a zigzaggy scar at the end of his eye
    Had Pirate Don Durk of Dowdee.

He kept in a cavern, this buccaneer bold,
A curious chest that was covered with mould,
And all of his pockets were jingly with gold!
    Oh jing! went the gold of Dowdee.

His conscience, of course, it was crook'd like a squash,
But both of his boots made a slickery slosh,
And he went through the world with a wonderful swash,
        Did Pirate Don Durk of Dowdee.

It's true he was wicked as wicked could be,
His sins they outnumbered a hundred and three,
But oh, he was perfectly gorgeous to see,
        The Pirate Don Durk of Dowdee.

—MILDRED PLEW MEIGS

How to Eat a Poem

Don't be polite.
Bite in.
Pick it up with your fingers and lick the juice that
       may run down your chin.
It is ready and ripe now, whenever you are.

You do not need a knife or fork or spoon
or plate or napkin or tablecloth.

For there is no core
or stem
or rind
or pit
or seed
or skin
to throw away.

                         —EVE MERRIAM

Fly

I have been cruel to a fat pigeon
Because he would not fly
All he wanted was to live like a friendly old man

He had let himself become a wreck filthy and confiding
Wild for his food beating the cat off the garbage
Ignoring his mate perpetually snotty at the beak
Smelling waddling having to be
Carried up the ladder at night content

Fly I said throwing him into the air
But he would drop and run back expecting to be fed
I said it again and again throwing him up
As he got worse
He let himself be picked up every time
Until I found him in the dovecote dead
Of the needless efforts

So that is what I am

Pondering his eye that could not
Conceive that I was a creature to run from

I who have always believed too much in words
                              —W.S. MERWIN

The Last One

Well they'd made up their minds to be everywhere because
      why not.
Everywhere was theirs because they thought so.
They with two leaves they whom the birds despise.
In the middle of stones they made up their minds.
They started to cut.

Well they cut everything because why not.
Everything was theirs because they thought so.
It fell into its shadows and they took both away.
Some to have some for burning.

Well cutting everything they came to the water.
They came to the end of the day there was one left standing.
They would cut it tomorrow they went away.
The night gathered in the last branches.
The shadow of the night gathered in the shadow of the water.
The night and the shadow put on the same head.
And it said Now.

Well in the morning they cut the last one.
Like the others the last one fell into its shadow.
It fell into its shadow on the water.
They took it away its shadow stayed on the water.

Well they shrugged they started trying to get the shadow away.
They cut right to the ground the shadow stayed whole.
They laid boards on it the shadow came out on top.
They shone lights on it the shadow got blacker and clearer.
They exploded the water the shadow rocked.
They built a huge fire on the roots.
They sent up black smoke between the shadow and the sun.
The new shadow flowed without changing the old one.
They shrugged they went away to get stones.

They came back the shadow was growing.
They started setting up stones it was growing.
They looked the other way it went on growing.

They decided they would make a stone out of it.
They took stones to the water they poured them into the shadow.
They poured them in they poured them in the stones vanished.
The shadow was not filled it went on growing.
That was one day.

The next day was just the same it went on growing.
They did all the same things it was just the same.
They decided to take its water from under it.
They took away water they took it away the water went down.
The shadow stayed where it was before.
It went on growing it grew onto the land.
They started to scrape the shadow with machines.
When it touched the machines it stayed on them.
They started to beat the shadow with sticks.
Where it touched the sticks it stayed on them.
They started to beat the shadow with hands.
Where it touched the hands it stayed on them.
That was another day.

Well the next day started about the same it went on growing.
They pushed lights into the shadow.
Where the shadow got onto them they went out.
They began to stomp on the edge it got their feet.
And when it got their feet they fell down.
It got into eyes the eyes went blind.

The ones that fell down it grew over and they vanished.
The ones that went blind and walked into it vanished.
The ones that could see and stood still
It swallowed their shadows.
Then it swallowed them too and they vanished.
Well the others ran.

The ones that were left went away to live if it would let them.
They went far as they could.
The lucky ones with their shadows.

—W.S. MERWIN

Afternoon on a Hill

I will be the gladdest thing
Under the sun!
I will touch a hundred flowers
and not pick one.

I will look at cliffs and clouds
with quiet eyes,
Watch the wind bow down the grass,
and the grass rise.

And when the lights begin to show
up from the town,
I will mark which must be mine,
and then start down!

—EDNA ST. VINCENT MILLAY

First Fig

My candle burns at both ends;
  It will not last the night;
But ah, my foes, and oh, my friends—
  It gives a lovely light!

—EDNA ST. VINCENT MILLAY

Recuerdo

We were very tired, we were very merry—
We had gone back and forth all night on the ferry.
It was bare and bright, and smelled like a stable—
But we looked into a fire, we leaned across a table,
We lay on the hill-top underneath the moon;
And the whistles kept blowing, and the dawn came soon.

We were very tired, we were very merry—
We had gone back and forth all night on the ferry;
And you ate an apple, and I ate a pear,
From a dozen of each we had bought somewhere;
And the sky went wan, and the wind came cold,
And the sun rose dripping, a bucketful of gold.

We were very tired, we were very merry—
We had gone back and forth all night on the ferry.
We hailed, "Good morrow, mother!" to a shawl-covered head,
And bought a morning paper, which neither of us read;
And she wept, "God bless you!" for the apples and the pears,
And we gave her all our money but our subway fares.

—EDNA ST. VINCENT MILLAY

Encounter

We were riding through frozen fields in a wagon at dawn.
A red wing rose in the darkness.

And suddenly a hare ran across the road.
One of us pointed to It wIth his hand.

That was long ago. Today neither of them is alive,
Not the hare, nor the man who made the gesture.

O my love, where are they, where are they going
The flash of a hand, streak of movement, rustle of pebbles.
I ask not out of sorrow, but in wonder.

—CZESLAW MILOSZ

The Sun

All colors come from the sun. And it does not have
Any particular color, for it contains them all.
And the whole Earth is like a poem
While the sun above represents the artist.

Whoever wants to paint the variegated world
Let him never look straight up at the sun
Or he will lose the memory of things he has seen.
Only burning tears will stay in his eyes.

Let him kneel down, lower his face to the grass,
And look at light reflected by the ground.
There he will find everything we have lost:
The stars and the roses, the dusks and the dawns.

—CZESLAW MILOSZ

A Visit from St. Nicholas

'Twas the night before Christmas, when all through the house
Not a creature was stirring, not even a mouse;
The stockings were hung by the chimney with care,
In hopes that St. Nicholas soon would be there;
The children were nestled all snug in their beds,
While visions of sugar-plums danced in their heads;
And mamma in her 'kerchief, and I in my cap,
Had just settled our brains for a long winter's nap—
When out on the lawn there arose such a clatter,
I sprang from my bed to see what was the matter.
Away to the window I flew like a flash,
Tore open the shutters and threw up the sash.
The moon, on the breast of the new-fallen snow,
Gave a lustre of midday to objects below;
When, what to my wondering eyes should appear,
But a miniature sleigh and eight tiny reindeer,
With a little old driver, so lively and quick,
I knew in a moment it must be St. Nick.
More rapid than eagles his coursers they came,
And he whistled, and shouted, and called them by name:
"Now, *Dasher*! now, *Dancer*! now *Prancer*! and *Vixen*!
On, *Comet*! on, *Cupid*! on *Donner* and *Blitzen*!
To the top of the porch! to the top of the wall!
Now dash away! dash away! dash away all!"
As dry leaves that before the wild hurricane fly,
When they meet with an obstacle, mount to the sky,
So up to the house-top the coursers they flew
With the sleigh full of toys, and St. Nicholas too.
And then, in a twinkling, I heard on the roof
The prancing and pawing of each little hoof—
As I drew in my head, and was turning around,
Down the chimney St. Nicholas came with a bound.
He was dressed all in fur, from his head to his foot,
And his clothes were all tarnished with ashes and soot;
A bundle of toys he had flung on his back,
And he looked like a pedlar just opening his pack.
His eyes—how they twinkled; his dimples, how merry!
His cheeks were like roses, his nose like a cherry!

His droll little mouth was drawn up like a bow,
And the beard of his chin was as white as the snow;
The stump of a pipe he held tight in his teeth,
And the smoke it encircled his head like a wreath;
He had a broad face and a little round belly,
That shook when he laughed, like a bowl full of jelly.
He was chubby and plump, a right jolly old elf,
And I laughed when I saw him, in spite of myself.
A wink of his eye and a twist of his head
Soon gave me to know I had nothing to dread;
He spoke not a word, but went straight to his work,
And filled all the stockings; then turned with a jerk,
And laying his finger aside of his nose,
And giving a nod, up the chimney he rose;
He sprang to his sleigh, to his team gave a whistle,
And away they all flew like the down of a thistle.
But I heard him exclaim, ere he drove out of sight,
"Happy Christmas to all, and to all a good night!"

—CLEMENT CLARKE MOORE

A Jelly-Fish

Visible, invisible,
    a fluctuating charm
an amber-tinctured amethyst
    inhabits it, your arm
approaches and it opens
    and it closes; you had meant
to catch it and it quivers;
    you abandon your intent.

—MARIANNE MOORE

I May, I Might, I Must

If you will tell me why the fen
appears impassable, I then
will tell you why I think that I
can get across it if I try.

—MARIANNE MOORE

Child's Song

I have a garden of my own,
    Shining with flowers of every hue;
I loved it dearly while alone,
    But I shall love it more with you:
And there the golden bees shall come,
    In summer time at break of morn,
And wake us with their busy hum
    Around the Siha's fragrant thorn.

I have a fawn from Aden's land,
    On leafy buds and berries nursed;
And you shall feed him from your hand,
    Though he may start with fear at first;
And I will lead you where he lies
    For shelter in the noon-tide heat;
And you may touch his sleeping eyes,
    And feel his little silvery feet.

—SIR THOMAS MOORE

The Minstrel Boy

The Minstrel Boy to the war is gone
    In the ranks of death you'll find him,
His father's sword he has girded on,
    And his wild harp slung behind him.
"Land of song!" sang the warrior bard,
    "Tho' all the world betrays thee,
One sword, at least, thy rights shall guard,
    One faithful harp shall praise thee."

The minstrel fell! but the foeman's chain
    Could not bring that proud soul under;
The harp he loved ne'er spoke again,
    For he tore its chords asunder;
And said, "No chain shall sully thee,
    Thou soul of love and bravery.
Thy songs were made for the pure and free,
    They shall never sound in slavery."

—SIR THOMAS MOORE

Animal Crackers

Animal crackers, and cocoa to drink,
That is the finest of suppers, I think;
When I'm grown up and can have what I please
I think I shall always insist upon these.

What do *you* choose when you're offered a treat?
When Mother says, "What would you like best to eat?"
Is it waffles and syrup, or cinnamon toast?
It's cocoa and animal crackers that *I* love most!

The kitchen's the cosiest place that I know:
The kettle is singing, the stove is aglow,
And there in the twilight, how jolly to see
The cocoa and animals waiting for me.

Daddy and Mother dine later in state,
With Mary to cook for them, Susan to wait;
But they don't have nearly as much fun as I
Who eat in the kitchen with Nurse standing by;
And Daddy once said, he would like to be me
Having cocoa and animals once more for tea!

—CHRISTOPHER MORLEY

The Plumpuppets

When little heads weary have gone to their bed,
When all the good nights and the prayers have been said,
Of all the good fairies that send bairns to rest
The little Plumpuppets are those I love best.

If your pillow is lumpy, or hot, thin, and flat,
The little Plumpuppets know just what they're at:
They plump up the pillow, all soft, cool, and fat—
The little Plumpuppets plump-up it!

The little Plumpuppets are fairies of beds;
They have nothing to do but to watch sleepyheads;
They turn down the sheets and they tuck you in tight,
And they dance on your pillow to wish you good night!

No matter what troubles have bothered the day,
Though your doll broke her arm or the pup ran away;
Though your handies are black with the ink that was spilt—
Plumpuppets are waiting in blanket and quilt.

If your pillow is lumpy, or hot, thin and flat,
The little Plumpuppets know just what they're at:
They plump up the pillow, all soft, cool, and fat—
The little Plumpuppets plump-up it!

—CHRISTOPHER MORLEY

The Wonder

Over my shoulder in Danbury, Connecticut, as I drove,
my father came back to wipe the rear window
and I could see, more clearly behind me than
in front, his one Studebaker dream but couldn't
smell the bakery in that so we walked from then on,
full of the smell; that was the wonder
of Wonder bread—we didn't have to buy any.

—THYLIAS MOSS

Experiment Degustatory

A gourmet challenged me to eat
A tiny bit of rattlesnake meat,
Remarking, "Don't look horror-stricken.
You'll find it tastes a lot like chicken."
It did.
Now chicken I cannot eat,
Because it tastes like rattlesnake meat.

—OGDEN NASH

The Parsnip

The parsnip, children, I repeat
Is simply an anemic beet.
Some people call the parsnip edible;
Myself, I find this claim incredible.

—OGDEN NASH

Adventures of Isabel

Isabel met an enormous bear;
Isabel, Isabel, didn't care.
The bear was hungry, the bear was ravenous,
The bear's big mouth was cruel and cavernous.
The bear said, Isabel, glad to meet you,
How do, Isabel, now I'll eat you!
Isabel, Isabel, didn't worry,
Isabel didn't scream or scurry.
She washed her hands and she straightened her hair up.
Then Isabel quietly ate the bear up.

Once on a night as black as pitch
Isabel met a wicked old witch.
The witch's face was cross and wrinkled,
The witch's gums with teeth were sprinkled.
Ho, ho, Isabel! the old witch crowed,
I'll turn you into an ugly toad!
Isabel, Isabel, didn't worry,
Isabel didn't scream or scurry.
She showed no rage and she showed no rancor,
But she turned the witch into milk and drank her.

Isabel met a hideous giant,
Isabel continued self-reliant.
The giant was hairy, the giant was horrid,
He had one eye in the middle of his forehead.
Good morning, Isabel, the giant said,
I'll grind your bones to make my bread.
Isabel, Isabel, didn't worry,
Isabel didn't scream or scurry.
She nibbled the zwieback that she always fed off,
And when it was gone, she cut the giant's head off.

Isabel met a troublesome doctor,
He punched and he poked till he really shocked her.
The doctor's talk was of coughs and chills
And the doctor's satchel bulged with pills.
The doctor said unto Isabel,

Swallow this, it will make you well.
Isabel, Isabel, didn't worry,
Isabel didn't scream or scurry.
She took those pills from the pill-concocter,
And Isabel calmly cured the doctor.

—OGDEN NASH

The Pit Ponies

They come like the ghosts of horses, shyly,
To this summer field, this fresh green,
Which scares them.

They have been too long in the blind mine,
Their hooves have trodden only stones
And the soft, thick dust of fine coal,

And they do not understand the grass.
For over two years their sun
Has shone from an electric bulb

That has never set, and their walking
Has been along the one, monotonous
Track of the pulled coal-trucks.

They have bunched their muscles against
The harness and pulled, and hauled.
But now they have come out of the underworld

And are set down in the sun and real air,
Which are strange to them. They are humble
And modest, their heads are downcast, they

Do not expect to see very far. But one
Is attempting a clumsy gallop. It is
Something he could do when he was very young,

When he was a little foal a long time ago
And he could run fleetly on his long foal's legs,
And almost he can remember this. And look,

One rolls on her back with joy in the clean grass!
And they all, awkwardly and hesitantly, like
Clumsy old men, begin to run, and the field

Is full of happy thunder. They toss their heads,
Their manes fly, they are galloping in freedom.
The ponies have come above ground, they are galloping!

—LESLIE NORRIS

Daddy Fell into the Pond

Everyone grumbled. The sky was grey.
We had nothing to do and nothing to say.
We were nearing the end of a dismal day,
And there seemed to be nothing beyond,
         THEN
    Daddy fell into the pond!

And everyone's face grew merry and bright,
And Timothy danced for sheer delight.
"Give me the camera, quick, oh quick!
He's crawling out of the duckweed."
Click!

Then the gardener suddenly slapped his knee,
And doubled up, shaking silently,
And the ducks all quacked as if they were daft
And it sounded as if the old drake laughed.

O, there wasn't a thing that didn't respond
         WHEN
    Daddy fell into the pond!

—ALFRED NOYES

The Highwayman

The wind was a torrent of darkness among the gusty trees,
The moon was a ghostly galleon tossed upon cloudy seas,
The road was a ribbon of moonlight over the purple moor,
And the highwayman came riding—
    Riding—riding—
The highwayman came riding, up to the old inn-door.

He'd a French cocked-hat on his forehead, a bunch of lace at his
    chin,
A coat of the claret velvet, and breeches of brown doe-skin;
They fitted with never a wrinkle; his boots were up to the thigh!
And he rode with a jeweled twinkle,
    His pistol butts a-twinkle,
His rapier hilt a-twinkle, under the jeweled sky.

Over the cobbles he clattered and clashed in the dark inn-yard,
And he tapped with his whip on the shutters, but all was locked
    and barred:
He whistled a tune to the window, and who should be waiting
    there
But the landlord's black-eyed daughter,
    Bess, the landlord's daughter,
Plaiting a dark red love-knot into her long black hair.

And dark in the dark old inn-yard a stable-wicket creaked
Where Tim the ostler listened; his face was white and peaked;
His eyes were hollows of madness, his hair like moldy hay,
But he loved the landlord's daughter,
    The landlord's red-lipped daughter,
Dumb as a dog he listened, and he heard the robber say—

"One kiss, my bonny sweetheart, I'm after a prize tonight,
But I shall be back with the yellow gold before the morning light;
Yet, if they press me sharply, and harry me through the day,
Then look for me by moonlight,
    Watch for me by moonlight,

I'll come to thee by moonlight, though hell should bar the way."

He rose upright in the stirrups; he scarce could reach her hand,
But she loosened her hair i' the casement! His face burned like a
    brand
As the black cascade of perfume came tumbling over his breast;
And he kissed its waves in the moonlight,
        (Oh, sweet black waves in the moonlight!)
Then he tugged at his rein in the moonlight, and galloped away to
    the West.

2

He did not come in the dawning; he did not come at noon;
And out o' the tawny sunset, before the rise o' the moon,
When the road was a gipsy's ribbon, looping the purple moor,
A red-coat troop came marching—
        Marching—marching—
King George's men came marching, up to the old inn-door.

They said no word to the landlord, they drank his ale instead,
But they gagged his daughter and bound her to the foot of her
    narrow bed;
Two of them knelt at her casement, with muskets at their side!
There was death at every window;
        And hell at one dark window;
For Bess could see, through her casement, the road that *he* would
    ride.

They had tied her up to attention, with many a sniggering jest;
They had bound a musket beside her, with the barrel beneath her
    breast!
"Now keep good watch!" and they kissed her. She heard the dead
    man say—
Look for me by moonlight;
    Watch for me by moonlight;
I'll come to thee by moonlight, though hell should bar the way!

She twisted her hands behind her; but all the knots held good!
She writhed her hands till her fingers were wet with sweat or
      blood!
They stretched and strained in the darkness, and the hours crawled
      by like years,
Till now, on the stroke of midnight,
      Cold, on the stroke of midnight,
The tip of one finger touched it! The trigger at least was hers!

The tip of one finger touched it; she strove no more for the rest!
Up, she stood up to attention, with the barrel beneath her breast,
She would not risk their hearing: she would not strive again;
For the road lay bare in the moonlight;
      Blank and bare in the moonlight;
And the blood of her veins in the moonlight throbbed to her love's
      refrain.

Tlot-tlot; tlot-tlot! Had they heard it? The horse-hoofs ringing
      clear;
Tlot-tlot; tlot-tlot,: in the distance? Were they deaf that they did
      not hear?
Down the ribbon of moonlight, over the brow of the hill,
The highwayman came riding,
      Riding, riding!
The red-coats looked to their priming! She stood up, straight and
      still!

Tlot-tlot, in the frosty silence! *Tlot-tlot,* in the echoing night!
Nearer he came and nearer! Her face was like a light!
Her eyes grew wide for a moment; she drew one last deep breath,
Then her finger moved in the moonlight,
      Her musket shattered the moonlight,
Shattered her breast in the moonlight and warned him—with her
      death.

He turned; he spurred to the westward; he did not know who stood
Bowed, with her head o'er the musket, drenched with her own red
      blood!

Not till the dawn he heard it, his face grew gray to hear
How Bess, the landlord's daughter,
        The landlord's black-eyed daughter,
Had watched for her love in the moonlight, and died in the darkness
        there.

Back he spurred like a madman, shrieking a curse to the sky,
With the white road smoking behind him, and his rapier brandished
        high!
Blood-red were his spurs in the golden moon; wine-red was his
        velvet coat,
When they shot him down on the highway,
        Down like a dog on the highway,
And he lay in his blood on the highway, with a bunch of lace at his
        throat.

. . . .

And still of a winter's night, they say, when the wind is in the trees,
When the moon is a ghostly galleon tossed upon cloudy seas,
When the road is a ribbon of moonlight over the purple moor,
A highwayman comes riding—
        Riding—riding—
A highwayman comes riding, up to the old inn-door.

Over the cobbles he clatters and clangs in the dark inn-yard;
And he taps with his whip on the shutters, but all is locked and
        barred;
He whistles a tune to the window, and who should be waiting there
        But the landlord's black-eyed daughter,
                Bess, the landlord's daughter,
        Plaiting a dark red love-knot into her long black hair.

                                        —ALFRED NOYES

What I Tell Him

I take my son outside
and show him a tree,
have him touch leaves,
this is a leaf, see,
it is green, it's got lines,
and it is shaped this way,
touch.
He touches the leaf
and branch trembles with his touch,
fat little hands roughly
and gently grasping what I show him.
Make him stand, bare feet,
on the ground, feel
that dirt, brown dirt and gravel,
solid clay, it won't grow seed
too well, have to have sand,
and leaves, sticks, manure,
and then it will grow things.
That's what I tell him.

—SIMON ORTIZ

Try, Try Again

'Tis a lesson you should heed,
    Try, try again;
If at first you don't succeed,
    Try, try again;
Then your courage should appear,
For, if you will persevere,
You will conquer, never fear;
    Try, try again.

        —T. H. PALMER

Snow Is Falling

Snow is falling, snow is falling.
Reaching for the storm's white stars,
Petals of geraniums stretch
Beyond the window bars.

Snow is falling all is chaos,
Everything is in the air,
The angle of the crossroads,
The steps of the back stair.

Snow is falling, not like flakes
But as if the firmament
In a coat with many patches
Were making its descent.

As if, from the upper landing,
Looking like a lunatic,
Creeping, playing hide-and-seek,
The sky stole from the attic.

Because life does not wait,
Turn, and you find Christmas here.
And a moment after that
It's suddenly New Year.

Snow is falling, thickly, thickly.
Keeping step, stride for stride,
No less quickly, nonchalantly,
Is that time, perhaps,
Passing in the street outside?

And perhaps year follows year
Like the snowflakes falling
Or the words that follow here?

Snow is falling, snow is falling,
Snow is falling, all is chaos:
The whitened ones who pass,
The angle of the crossroads,
The dazed plants by the glass.

— BORIS PASTERNAK
Translated by Jon
Stallworthy and
Peter France

Exclamation

Stillness
        not on the branch
in the air
        Not in the air
in the moment
        hummingbird

—OCTAVIO PAZ
Translated by
Eliot Weinberger

from The Bed Book

Most Beds are Beds
For sleeping or resting,
But the *best* Beds are much
More interesting!

Not just a white little
Tucked-in-tight little
Nighty-night little
Turn-out-the-light little
      Bed—

      Instead
A Bed for Fishing,
A Bed for Cats,
A Bed for a Troupe of
        Acrobats.

The *right* sort of Bed
(If you see what I mean)
Is a Bed that might
Be a Submarine

Nosing through water
Clear and green,
Silver and glittery
As a sardine.

Or a Jet-Propelled Bed
For visiting Mars
With mosquito nets
For the shooting stars. . . .
   . . . .

             —SYLVIA PLATH

Giraffe

The only head in the sky.
Buoyed like a bird's,
on bird legs too.
Moves in the slow motion
of a ride
across the longlegged miles
of the same place.
Grazes in trees.
Bends like a bow
over water
in a shy sort of
spreadeagle.
Embarrassed by
such vulnerability,
often trembles, gathering
together
in a single moment
the whole loose
fragment of body
before the run downwind.
Will stand still
in a camouflage of kind
in a rare daylight
for hours,
the leaves spilling
one break of sun
into another,
listening to the lions.
Will, when dark comes
and the fields open
until there are
no fields,
turn in the length
of light
toward some calm
still part of a tree's
new shadow, part of the moon.

Will stand all night
so tall
the sun will rise.

—STANLEY PLUMLY

Annabel Lee

It was many and many a year ago,
    In a kingdom by the sea
That a maiden there lived, whom you may know
    By the name of Annabel Lee;
And this maiden she lived with no other thought
    Than to love and be loved by me.

I was a child and *she* was a child,
    In this kingdom by the sea,
But we loved with a love that was more than love—
    I and my Annabel Lee—
With a love that the wingèd seraphs of heaven
    Coveted her and me.

And this was the reason that, long ago,
    In this kingdom by the sea,
A wind blew out of a cloud, chilling
    My beautiful Annabel Lee;
So that her highborn kinsmen came
    And bore her away from me,
To shut her up in a sepulcher
    In this kingdom by the sea.

The angels, not half so happy in heaven,
    Went envying her and me—
Yes!—that was the reason (as all men know,
    In this kingdom by the sea)
That the wind came out of the cloud by night,
    Chilling and killing my Annabel Lee.

But our love it was stronger by far than the love
    Of those who were older than we—
    Of many far wiser than we—
And neither the angels in heaven above,
    Nor the demons down under the sea,
Can ever dissever my soul from the soul
    Of the beautiful Annabel Lee:

For the moon never beams, without bringing me dreams
    Of the beautiful Annabel Lee;
And the stars never rise, but I feel the bright eyes
    Of the beautiful Annabel Lee:
And so, all the night-tide, I lie down by the side
Of my darling—my darling—my life and my bride,
    In the sepulcher there by the sea—
    In her tomb by the sounding sea.

—EDGAR ALLAN POE

The Raven

Once upon a midnight dreary, while I pondered, weak and weary,
Over many a quaint and curious volume of forgotten lore—
While I nodded, nearly napping, suddenly there came a tapping,
As of some one gently rapping, rapping at my chamber door—
"'Tis some visitor," I muttered, "tapping at my chamber door—
      Only this and nothing more."

Ah, distinctly I remember it was in the bleak December;
And each separate dying ember wrought its ghost upon the floor.
Eagerly I wished the morrow;—vainly I had sought to borrow
From my books surcease of sorrow—sorrow for the lost Lenore—
For the rare and radiant maiden whom the angels name Lenore—
      Nameless *here* for evermore.

And the silken, sad, uncertain rustling of each purple curtain
Thrilled me—filled me with fantastic terrors never felt before;
So that now, to still the beating of my heart, I stood repeating
"'Tis some visitor entreating entrance at my chamber door—
Some late visitor entreating entrance at my chamber door;—
      This it is and nothing more."

Presently my soul grew stronger; hesitating then no longer,
"Sir," said I, "or Madam, truly your forgiveness I implore;
But the fact is I was napping, and so gently you came rapping,
And so faintly you came tapping, tapping at my chamber door,
That I scarce was sure I heard you"—here I opened wide the
      door;—
      Darkness there and nothing more.

Deep into that darkness peering, long I stood there wondering,
      fearing,
Doubting, dreaming dreams no mortal ever dared to dream before;
But the silence was unbroken, and the stillness gave no token,
And the only word there spoken was the whispered word,
      "Lenore?"
This I whispered, and an echo murmured back the word,
      "Lenore!"
      Merely this and nothing more.

Back into the chamber turning, all my soul within me burning,
Soon again I heard a tapping somewhat louder than before.
"Surely," said I, "surely that is something at my window lattice;
Let me see, then, what thereat is, and this mystery explore—
Let my heart be still a moment and this mystery explore;—
        'Tis the wind and nothing more!"

Open here I flung the shutter, when, with many a flirt and flutter,
In there stepped a stately Raven of the saintly days of yore;
Not the least obeisance made he; not a minute stopped or stayed
        he;
But, with mien of lord or lady, perched above my chamber door—
Perched upon a bust of Pallas just above my chamber door—
        Perched, and sat, and nothing more.

Then this ebony bird beguiling my sad fancy into smiling,
By the grave and stern decorum of the countenance it wore,
"Though thy crest be shorn and shaven, thou," I said, "art sure no
        craven,
Ghastly grim and ancient Raven wandering from the Nightly
        shore—
Tell me what thy lordly name is on the Night's Plutonian shore!"
        Quoth the Raven "Nevermore."

Much I marvelled this ungainly fowl to hear discourse so plainly,
Though its answer little meaning—little relevancy bore;
For we cannot help agreeing that no living human being
Ever yet was blessed with seeing bird above his chamber door—
Bird or beast upon the sculptured bust above his chamber door,
        With such a name as "Nevermore."

But the Raven, sitting lonely on the placid bust, spoke only
That one word, as if his soul in that one word he did outpour.
Nothing farther then he uttered—not a feather then he fluttered—
Till I scarcely more than muttered "Other friends have flown
        before—
On the morrow he will leave me, as my Hopes have flown before."
        Then the bird said "Nevermore."

Startled at the stillness broken by reply so aptly spoken,
"Doubtless," said I, "what it utters is its only stock and store
Caught from some unhappy master whom unmerciful Disaster
Followed fast and followed faster till his songs one burden bore
'Till the dirges of his Hope that melancholy burden bore
    Of 'Never—nevermore.'"

But the Raven still beguiling my sad fancy into smiling,
Straight I wheeled a cushioned seat in front of bird, and bust and
        door;
Then, upon the velvet sinking, I betook myself to linking
Fancy unto fancy, thinking what this ominous bird of yore—
What this grim, ungainly, ghastly, gaunt, and ominous bird of yore
    Meant in croaking "Nevermore."

This I sat engaged in guessing, but no syllable expressing
To the fowl whose fiery eyes now burned into my bosom's core;
This and more I sat divining, with my head at ease reclining
On the cushion's velvet lining that the lamp-light gloated o'er,
But whose velvet-violet lining with the lamp-light gloating o'er,
    She shall press, ah, nevermore!

Then, methought, the air grew denser, perfumed from an unseen
        censer
Swung by seraphim whose foot-falls tinkled on the tufted floor.
"Wretch," I cried, "thy God hath lent thee—by these angels he
        hath sent thee
Respite—respite and nepenthe from thy memories of Lenore;
Quaff, oh quaff this kind nepenthe and forget this lost Lenore!"
    Quoth the Raven "Nevermore."

"Prophet!" said I, "thing of evil!—prophet still, if bird or devil!—
Whether Tempter sent, or whether tempest tossed thee here ashore,
Desolate yet all undaunted, on this desert land enchanted—
On this home by Horror haunted—tell me truly, I implore—
Is there—*is* there balm in Gilead?—tell me—tell me, I implore!"
    Quoth the Raven "Nevermore."

"Prophet!" said I, "thing of evil!—prophet still, if bird or devil!
By that Heaven that bends above us—by that God we both
        adore—
Tell this soul with sorrow laden if, within the distant Aidenn,
It shall clasp a sainted maiden whom the angels name Lenore—
Clasp a rare and radiant maiden whom the angels name Lenore."
        Quoth the Raven "Nevermore."

"Be that word our sign of parting, bird or fiend!" I shrieked,
        upstarting—
"Get thee back into the tempest and the Night's Plutonian shore!
Leave no black plume as a token of that lie thy soul hath spoken!
Leave my loneliness unbroken!—quit the bust above my door!
Take thy beak from out my heart, and take thy form from off my
        door!"
        Quoth the Raven "Nevermore."

And the Raven, never flitting, still is sitting, *still* is sitting
On the pallid bust of Pallas just above my chamber door;
And his eyes have all the seeming of a demon's that is dreaming,
And the lamp-light o'er him streaming throws his shadow on the
        floor;
And my soul from out that shadow that lies floating on the floor
        Shall be lifted—nevermore!

        —EDGAR ALLAN POE

The Bells

1

Hear the sledges with the bells—
Silver bells!
What a world of merriment their melody foretells!
How they tinkle, tinkle, tinkle.
In the icy air of night!
While the stars that oversprinkle
All the Heavens, seem to twinkle
With a crystalline delight;
Keeping time, time, time,
In a sort of Runic rhyme,
To the tintinabulation that so musically wells
From the bells, bells, bells, bells,
Bells, bells, bells—
From the jingling and the tinkling of the bells.

2

Hear the mellow wedding bells—
Golden bells!
What a world of happiness their harmony foretells!
Through the balmy air of night
How they ring out their delight!—
From the molten-golden notes
And all in tune,
What a liquid ditty floats
To the turtle-dove that listens while she gloats
On the moon!
Oh, from out the sounding cells
What a gush of euphony voluminously wells!
How it swells!
How it dwells
On the Future!—how it tells
Of the rapture that impels
To the swinging and the ringing
Of the bells, bells, bells!—
Of the bells, bells, bells, bells,

Bells, bells, bells—
To the rhyming and the chiming of the bells!

3

Hear the loud alarum bells—
Brazen bells!
What tale of terror, now, their turbulency tells!
In the startled ear of Night
How they scream out their affright!
Too much horrified to speak,
They can only shriek, shriek,
Out of tune,
In a clamorous appealing to the mercy of the fire—
In a mad expostulation with the deaf and frantic fire,
Leaping higher, higher, higher,
With a desperate desire
And a resolute endeavor
Now—now to sit, or never,
By the side of the pale-faced moon.
Oh, the bells, bells, bells!
What a tale their terror tells
Of despair!
How they clang and clash and roar!
What a horror they outpour
In the bosom of the palpitating air!
Yet the ear, it fully knows,
By the twanging
And the clanging,
How the danger ebbs and flows:—
Yes, the ear distinctly tells,
In the jangling
And the wrangling,
How the danger sinks and swells,
By the sinking or the swelling in the anger of the bells—
Of the bells—
Of the bells, bells, bells, bells,
Bells, bells, bells—

In the clamor and the clangor of the bells.

4

Hear the tolling of the bells—
      Iron bells!
What a world of solemn thought their monody compels!
      In the silence of the night
      How we shiver with affright
   At the melancholy meaning of the tone!
      For every sound that floats
      From the rust within their throats
         Is a groan.
      And the people—ah, the people
      They that dwell up in the steeple
         All alone,
      And who, tolling, tolling, tolling,
         In that muffled monotone,
      Feel a glory in so rolling
         On the human heart a stone—
They are neither man nor woman—
They are neither brute nor human,
         They are Ghouls:—
And their king it is who tolls:—
And he rolls, rolls, rolls, rolls
         A Pæan from the bells!
      And his merry bosom swells
         With the Pæan of the bells!
      And he dances and he yells;
Keeping time, time, time,
In a sort of Runic rhyme,
         To the Pæan of the bells—
            Of the bells:—
Keeping time, time, time,
In a sort of Runic rhyme,
         To the throbbing of the bells—
Of the bells, bells, bells—
         To the sobbing of the bells:—

Keeping time, time, time,
    As he knells, knells, knells,
In a happy Runic rhyme,
    To the rolling of the bells—
Of the bells, bells, bells:—
    To the tolling of the bells—
Of the bells, bells, bells, bells,
    Bells, bells, bells—
To the moaning and the groaning of the bells.

—EDGAR ALLAN POE

Eldorado

Gaily bedight,
A gallant knight,
In sunshine and in shadow,
Had journeyed long,
Singing a song,
In search of Eldorado.

But he grew old—
This knight so bold—
And o'er his heart a shadow
Fell as he found
No spot of ground
That looked like Eldorado.

And, as his strength
Failed him at length,
He met a pilgrim shadow—
"Shadow," said he,
"Where can it be—
This land of Eldorado?"

"Over the Mountains
Of the Moon,
Down the Valley of the Shadow,
Ride, boldly ride,"
The shade replied,—
"If you seek for Eldorado!"

—EDGAR ALLAN POE

In a Station of the Metro

The apparition of these faces in the crowd;
Petals on a wet, black bough.

—EZRA POUND

The Little Box

The little box gets her first teeth
And her little length
Little width little emptiness
And all the rest she has

The little box continues growing
The cupboard that she was inside
Is now inside her

And she grows bigger bigger bigger
Now the room is inside her
And the house and the city and the earth
And the world she was in before

The little box remembers her childhood
And by a great great longing
She becomes a little box again

Now in the little box
You have the whole world in miniature
You can easily put it in a pocket
Easily steal it easily lose it

Take care of the little box

—VASKO POPA
Translated by
Charles Simic.

The Spaghetti Nut

Eddie the spaghetti nut
courted pretty Nettie Cutt.
They wed and Ed and Nettie got
a cottage in Connecticut.

Eddie said to Nettie, "Hot
spaghetti I've just got to get."
So Nettie put it in a pot
and cooked spaghetti hot and wet.

Nettie cut spaghetti up
for Eddie in Connecticut.
Eddie slurped it from a cup,
that hot spaghetti Nettie cut.

Then Eddie, Nettie and their cat
that Nettie called Spaghettipet
all sat in the spaghetti vat—
so much for their spaghettiquette.

—JACK PRELUTSKY

Homework! Oh, Homework!

Homework! Oh, homework!
I hate you! You stink!
I wish I could wash you
away in the sink,
if only a bomb
would explode you to bits.
Homework! Oh, homework!
You're giving me fits.

I'd rather take baths
with a man-eating shark,
or wrestle a lion
alone in the dark,
eat spinach and liver,
pet ten porcupines,
than tackle the homework
my teacher assigns.

Homework! Oh, homework!
You're last on my list,
I simply can't see
why you even exist,
if you just disappeared
it would tickle me pink.
Homework! Oh, homework!
I hate you! You stink!

—JACK PRELUTSKY

Little Orphant Annie

Little Orphant Annie's come to our house to stay,
An' wash the cups and saucers up, an' brush the crumbs away,
An' shoo the chickens off the porch, an' dust the hearth, an'
      sweep,
An' make the fire, an' bake the bread, an' earn her board-an'-keep;
An' all us other children, when the supper things is done,
We set around the kitchen fire an' has the mostest fun
A-list'nin' to the witch tales 'at Annie tells about,
An' the Gobble-uns 'at gits you
        Ef you
            Don't
                Watch
                    Out!

Onc't they was a little boy wouldn't say his prayers,—
So when he went to bed at night, away upstairs,
His Mammy heerd him holler, an' his Daddy heerd him bawl,
An' when they turn't the kivvers down, he wasn't there at all!
An' they seeked him in the rafter room, an' cubbyhole, an' press,
An' seeked him up the chimbly flue, an' ever'wheres, I guess;
But all they ever found was thist his pants an' roundabout:—
An' the Gobble-uns 'll git you
        Ef you
            Don't
                Watch
                    Out!

An' one time a little girl 'ud allus laugh an' grin,
An' make fun of ever'one, an' all her blood an' kin;
An' onc't, when they was "company," an' ole folks was there,
She mocked 'em an' shocked 'em, an' said she didn't care!
An' thist as she kicked her heels, an' turn't to run an' hide,
They was two great big Black Things a-standin' by her side,
An' they snatched her through the ceilin' 'fore she knowed what
      she's about!
An' the Gobble-uns 'll git you
        Ef you
            Don't
                Watch
                    Out!

An' little Orphant Annie says, when the blaze is blue,
An' the lamp-wick sputters, an' the wind goes *woo-oo!*
An' you hear the crickets quit, an' the moon is gray,
An' the lightnin' bugs in dew is all squenched away,—
You better mind yer parents, and yer teachers fond an' dear,
An' churish them 'at loves you, an' dry the orphant's tear,
An' he'p the pore an' needy ones 'at clusters all about,
Er the Gobble-uns 'll git you
        Ef you
     Don't
        Watch
           Out!
              —JAMES WHITCOMB RILEY

Richard Cory

Whenever Richard Cory went down town,
We people on the pavement looked at him:
He was a gentleman from sole to crown,
Clean favored, and imperially slim.

And he was always quietly arrayed,
And he was always human when he talked;
But still he fluttered pulses when he said,
"Good-morning," and he glittered when he walked.

And he was rich—yes, richer than a king—
And admirably schooled in every grace:
In fine, we thought that he was everything
To make us wish that we were in his place.

So on we worked, and waited for the light,
And went without the meat, and cursed the bread;
And Richard Cory, one calm summer night,
Went home and put a bullet through his head.

                              —EDWIN ARLINGTON ROBINSON

Miniver Cheevy

Miniver Cheevy, child of scorn,
        Grew lean while he assailed the seasons;
He wept that he was ever born,
        And he had reasons.

Miniver loved the days of old
        When swords were bright and steeds were prancing;
The vision of a warrior bold
        Would set him dancing.

Miniver sighed for what was not,
        And dreamed, and rested from his labors;
He dreamed of Thebes and Camelot,
        And Priam's neighbors.

Miniver mourned the ripe renown
        That made so many a name so fragrant;
He mourned Romance, now on the town,
        And Art, a vagrant.

Miniver loved the Medici,
        Albeit he had never seen one;
He would have sinned incessantly
        Could he have been one.

Miniver cursed the commonplace
        And eyed a khaki suit with loathing;
He missed the mediæval grace
        Of iron clothing.

Miniver scorned the gold he sought,
        But sore annoyed was he without it;
Miniver thought, and thought, and thought,
        And thought about it.

Miniver Cheevy, born too late,
    Scratched his head and kept on thinking;
Miniver coughed, and called it fate,
    And kept on drinking.

—EDWIN ARLINGTON ROBINSON

The Lady and the Bear

A Lady came to a Bear by a Stream.
"O why are you fishing that way?
Tell me, dear Bear there by the Stream,
Why are you fishing that way?"

"I am what is known as a Biddly Bear,—
That's why I'm fishing this way.
We Biddly's are Pee-culiar Bears.
And so,—I'm fishing this way.

"And besides, it seems there's a Law:
A most, most exactious Law
Says a Bear
Doesn't dare
Doesn't dare
Doesn't DARE
Use a Hook or a Line,
Or an old piece of Twine,
Not even the end of his Claw, Claw, Claw,
Not even the end of his Claw.
Yes, a Bear has to fish with his Paw, Paw, Paw.
A Bear has to fish with his Paw."

"O it's Wonderful how with a flick of your Wrist,
You can fish out a fish, out a fish, out a fish,
If *I* were a fish I just couldn't resist
You, when you are fishing that way, that way,
When you are fishing that way."

And at that the Lady slipped from the Bank
And fell in the Stream still clutching a Plank,
But the Bear just sat there until she Sank;
As he went on fishing his way, his way,
As he went on fishing his way.

—THEODORE ROETHKE

The Bat

By day the bat is cousin to the mouse.
He likes the attic of an aging house.

His fingers make a hat about his head.
His pulse beat is so slow we think him dead.

He loops in crazy figures half the night
Among the trees that face the corner light.

But when he brushes up against a screen,
We are afraid of what our eyes have seen:

For something is amiss or out of place
When mice with wings can wear a human face.

—THEODORE ROETHKE

The Sloth

In moving-slow he has no Peer.
You ask him something in his ear;
He thinks about it for a Year;

And, then, before he says a Word
There, upside down (unlike a Bird)
He will assume that you have Heard—

A most Ex-as-per-at-ing Lug.
But should you call his manner Smug,
He'll sigh and give his Branch a Hug;

Then off again to Sleep he goes,
Still swaying gently by his Toes,
And you just know he knows he knows.

            —THEODORE ROETHKE

My Papa's Waltz

The whisky on your breath
Could make a small boy dizzy;
But I hung on like death:
Such waltzing was not easy.

We romped until the pans
Slid from the kitchen shelf;
My mother's countenance
Could not unfrown itself.

The hand that held my wrist
Was battered on one knuckle;
At every step you missed
My right ear scraped a buckle.

You beat time on my head
With a palm caked hard by dirt,
Then waltzed me off to bed
Still clinging to your shirt.

—THEODORE ROETHKE

The Meadow Mouse

1

In a shoe box stuffed in an old nylon stocking
Sleeps the baby mouse I found in the meadow,
Where he trembled and shook beneath a stick
Till I caught him up by the tail and brought him in,
Cradled in my hand,
A little quaker, the whole body of him trembling,
His absurd whiskers sticking out like a cartoon-mouse,
His feet like small leaves,
Little lizard-feet,
Whitish and spread wide when he tried to struggle away,
Wriggling like a miniscule puppy.

Now he's eaten his three kinds of cheese and drunk from his
        bottle-cap watering-trough—
So much he just lies in one corner,
His tail curled under him, his belly big
As his head; his bat-like ears
Twitching, tilting toward the least sound.

Do I imagine he no longer trembles
When I come close to him?
He seems no longer to tremble.

2

But this morning the shoe-box house on the back porch is empty.
Where has he gone, my meadow mouse,
My thumb of a child that nuzzled in my palm?—
To run under the hawk's wing,
Under the eye of the great owl watching from the elm-tree,
To live by courtesy of the shrike, the snake, the tom-cat.

I think of the nestling fallen into the deep grass,
The turtle gasping in the dusty rubble of the highway,
The paralytic stunned in the tub, and the water rising,—
All things innocent, hapless, forsaken.

—THEODORE ROETHKE

The Monotony Song

A donkey's tail is very nice
You mustn't pull it more than twice,
Now that's a piece of good advice
     —Heigho, meet Hugh and Harry!

One day Hugh walked up to a bear
And said, Old Boy, you're shedding hair,
And shedding more than here and there,
     —Heigho, we're Hugh and Harry!

The bear said, Sir, you go too far,
I wonder who you think you are
To make remarks about my—Grrrr!
     —And there was only Harry!

This Harry ran straight up a wall,
But found he wasn't there at all,
And so he had a horrid fall.
     —Alas, alack for Harry!

My sweetheart is an ugly witch,
And you should see her noses twitch,—
But Goodness Me, her father's rich!
     —And I'm not Hugh nor Harry!

This is, you see, a silly song
And you can sing it all day long—
You'll find I'm either right or wrong
     —Heigho Hugh and Harry!

The moral is, I guess you keep
Yourself awake until you sleep,
And sometimes look before you leap
     —Unless you're Hugh or Harry!
             —THEODORE ROETHKE

Caterpillar

Brown and furry
Caterpillar in a hurry,
Take your walk
To the shady leaf, or stalk,
Or what not,
Which may be the chosen spot.
No toad spy you,
Hovering bird of prey pass by you;
Spin and die,
To live again a butterfly.

—CHRISTINA ROSSETTI

Who Has Seen the Wind?

Who has seen the wind?
    Neither I nor you:
But when the leaves hang trembling,
    The wind is passing through.

Who has seen the wind?
    Neither you nor I:
But when the trees bow down their heads,
    The wind is passing by.

—CHRISTINA ROSSETTI

Precious Stones

An emerald is as green as grass,
    A ruby red as blood,
A sapphire shines as blue as heaven,
    But a flint lies in the mud.

A diamond is a brilliant stone
    To catch the world's desire,
An opal holds a rainbow light,
    But a flint holds fire.

            —CHRISTINA ROSSETTI

Remember

Remember me when I am gone away,
Gone far away into the silent land;
When you can no more hold me by the hand,
Nor I half turn to go, yet turning stay.
Remember me when no more, day by day,
You tell me of our future that you planned:
Only remember me; you understand
It will be late to counsel then or pray.

Yet if you should forget me for a while
And afterwards remember, do no grieve;
For if the darkness and corruption leave
A vestige of the thoughts that once I had,
Better by far you should forget and smile
Than that you should remember and be sad.

—CHRISTINA ROSSETTI

What Is Pink?

What is pink? A rose is pink
By the fountain's brink.
What is red? A poppy's red
In its barley bed.
What is blue? The sky is blue
Where the clouds float thro'.
What is white? A swan is white
Sailing in the light.
What is yellow? Pears are yellow,
Rich and ripe and mellow.
What is green? The grass is green,
With small flowers between.
What is violet? Clouds are violet
In the summer twilight.
What is orange? Why, an orange,
Just an orange!

—CHRISTINA ROSSETTI

Transformations

My little son enters
the room and says
"you are a vulture
I am a mouse"

I put away my book
wings and claws
grow out of me

their ominous shadows
race on the walls
I am a vulture
he is a mouse

"you are a wolf
I am a goat"
I walk around the table
and am a wolf
windowpanes gleam
like fangs
in the dark
while he runs to his mother
safe
his head hidden in the warmth of her dress

—TADEUSZ RÓZEWICZ
Translated by Czesław
Miłosz

Ballad of Orange and Grape

After you finish your work
after you do your day
after you've read your reading
after you've written your say —
you go down the street to the hot dog stand,
one block down and across the way.
On a blistering afternoon in East Harlem in the twentieth century.

Most of the windows are boarded up,
the rats run out of a sack —
sticking out of the crummy garage
one shiny long Cadillac;
at the glass door of the drug-addiction center,
a man who'd like to break your back.
But here's a brown woman with a little girl dressed in rose and
        pink, too.

Frankfurters frankfurters sizzle on the steel
where the hot-dog-man leans —
nothing else on the counter
but the usual two machines,
the grape one, empty, and the orange one, empty,
I face him in between.
A black boy comes along, looks at the hot dogs, goes on walking.

I watch the man as he stands and pours
in the familiar shape
bright purple in the one marked ORANGE
orange in the one marked grape,
the grape drink in the machine marked ORANGE
and orange drink in the GRAPE.
Just the one word large and clear, unmistakeable, on each
        machine.

I ask him : How can we go on reading
and make sense out of what we read? —

How can they write and believe what they're writing,
the young ones across the street,
while you go on pouring grape into orange
and orange into the one marked grape —?
(How are we going to believe what we read and we write and we
        hear and we say and we do?)

He looks at the two machines and he smiles
and he shrugs and smiles and pours again.
It could be violence and nonviolence
it could be white and black   women and men
it could be war and peace or any
binary system, love and hate, enemy, friend.
Yes and no, be and not-be, what we do and what we don't
        do.

On a corner in East Harlem
garbage, reading, a deep smile, rape,
forgetfulness, a hot street of murder,
misery, withered hope,
a man keeps pouring grape into ORANGE
and orange into the one marked GRAPE,
pouring orange into GRAPE and grape into ORANGE forever.

—MURIEL RUKEYSER

The Message of the Rain

when i was a child
i was a squirrel a bluejay a fox
and spoke with them in their tongues
climbed their trees dug their dens
and knew the taste
of every grass and stone
the meaning of the sun
the message of the night

now i am old and past
both work and battle
and know no shame
to go alone into the forest
to speak again to squirrel fox and bird
to taste the world
to find the meaning of the wind
the message of the rain

—NORMAN H. RUSSELL

Fog

The fog comes
on little cat feet.

It sits looking
over harbor and city
on silent haunches
and then moves on.

—CARL SANDBURG

Buffalo Dusk

The buffaloes are gone.
And those who saw the buffaloes are gone.
Those who saw the buffaloes by thousands and how they
       pawed the prairie sod into dust with their great hoofs,
       their great heads down pawing on in a great pageant
       of dusk,
Those who saw the buffaloes are gone.
And the buffaloes are gone.

—CARL SANDBURG

Lochinvar

O, young Lochinvar is come out of the west,
Through all the wide Border his steed was the best,
And save his good broadsword he weapons had none;
He rode all unarmed, and he rode all alone.
So faithful in love, and so dauntless in war,
There never was knight like the young Lochinvar.

He stayed not for brake, and he stopped not for stone,
He swam the Eske river where ford there was none;
But, ere he alighted at Netherby gate,
The bride had consented, the gallant came late:
For a laggard in love, and a dastard in war,
Was to wed the fair Ellen of brave Lochinvar.

So boldly he entered the Netherby hall,
Among bride's-men and kinsmen, and brothers and all;
Then spoke the bride's father, his hand on his sword
(For the poor craven bridegroom said never a word),
"O come ye in peace here, or come ye in war,
Or to dance at our bridal, young Lord Lochinvar?"

"I long wooed your daughter, my suit you denied;—
Love swells like the Solway, but ebbs like its tide—
And now I am come, with this lost love of mine,
To lead but one measure, drink one cup of wine.
There are maidens in Scotland more lovely by far,
That would gladly be bride to the young Lochinvar."

The bride kissed the goblet; the knight took it up,
He quaffed off the wine, and he threw down the cup,
She looked down to blush, and she looked up to sigh,
With a smile on her lips and a tear in her eye.
He took her soft hand, ere her mother could bar,—
"Now tread we a measure!" said young Lochinvar.

So stately his form, and so lovely her face,
That never a hall such a galliard did grace;
While her mother did fret, and her father did fume,

And the bridegroom stood dangling his bonnet and plume;
And the bride-maidens whispered, "'Twere better by far
To have matched our fair cousin with young Lochinvar."

One touch to her hand, and one word in her ear,
When they reached the hall door, and the charger stood near;
So light to the croupe the fair lady he swung,
So light to the saddle before her he sprung!
"She is won! we are gone, over bank, bush, and scaur;
They'll have fleet steeds that follow," quoth young Lochinvar.

There was mounting 'mong Græmes of the Netherby clan;
Forsters, Fenwicks, and Musgraves, they rode and they ran;
There was racing, and chasing, on Cannobie Lee,
But the lost bride of Netherby ne'er did they see.
So daring in love, and so dauntless in war,
Have ye e'er heard of gallant like young Lochinvar?

—SIR WALTER SCOTT

The Cremation of Sam McGee

There are strange things done in the midnight sun
By the men who moil for gold;
The Arctic trails have their secret tales
That would make your blood run cold;
The Northern Lights have seen queer sights,
But the queerest they ever did see
Was that night on the marge of Lake Lebarge
I cremated Sam McGee.

Now Sam McGee was from Tennessee, where the cotton blooms
and blows.
Why he left his home in the South to roam 'round the Pole,
God only knows.
He was always cold, but the land of gold seemed to hold him like
a spell;
Though he'd often say in his homely way that "he'd sooner live
in hell."

On a Christmas Day we were mushing our way over the Daw-
son trail.
Talk of your cold! through the parka's fold it stabbed like a
driven nail.
If our eyes we'd close, then the lashes froze till sometimes we
couldn't see;
It wasn't much fun, but the only one to whimper was Sam
McGee.

And that very night, as we lay packed tight in our robes be-
neath the snow,
And the dogs were fed, and the stars o'erhead were dancing
heel and toe,
He turned to me, and "Cap," says he, "I'll cash in this trip, I
guess;
And if I do, I'm asking that you won't refuse my last request."

Well, he seemed so low that I couldn't say no; then he says with
a sort of moan:
"It's the cursèd cold, and it's got right hold till I'm chilled clean

through to the bone.
Yet 'tain't being dead—it's my awful dread of the icy grave
that pains;
So I want you to swear that, foul or fair, you'll cremate my last
remains."

A pal's last need is a thing to heed, so I swore I would not fail;
And we started on at the streak of dawn; but God! he looked
ghastly pale.
He crouched on the sleigh, and he raved all day of his home in
Tennessee;
And before nightfall a corpse was all that was left of Sam McGee.

There wasn't a breath in that land of death, and I hurried, horror-
driven,
With a corpse half hid that I couldn't get rid, because of a
promise given;
It was lashed to the sleigh, and it seemed to say: "You may tax
your brawn and brains,
But you promised true, and it's up to you to cremate those last
remains."

Now a promise made is a debt unpaid, and the trail has its own
stern code.
In the days to come, though my lips were dumb, in my heart
how I cursed that load.
In the long, long night, by the lone firelight, while the huskies,
round in a ring,
Howled out their woes to the homeless snows—O God! how
I loathed the thing.

And every day that quiet clay seemed to heavy and heavier
grow;
And on I went, though the dogs were spent and the grub was
getting low;
The trail was bad, and I felt half mad, but I swore I would not
give in;

And I'd often sing to the hateful thing, and it hearkened with
    a grin.

Till I came to the marge of Lake Lebarge, and a derelict there lay;
It was jammed in the ice, but I saw in a trice it was called the
        "Alice May."
And I looked at it, and I thought a bit, and I looked at my frozen
        chum;
Then "Here," said I, with sudden cry, "is my cre-ma-tor-eum."

Some planks I tore from the cabin floor, and I lit the boiler fire;
Some coal I found that was lying around, and I heaped the fuel
        higher;
The flames just soared, and the furnace roared—such a blaze you
        seldom see;
And I burrowed a hole in the glowing coal, and I stuffed in
        Sam McGee.

Then I made a hike, for I didn't like to hear him sizzle so;
And the heavens scowled, and the huskies howled, and the wind
        began to blow.
It was icy cold, but the hot sweat rolled down my cheeks, and I
        don't know why;
And the greasy smoke in an inky cloak went streaking down
        the sky.

I do not know how long in the snow I wrestled with grisly fear;
But the stars came out and they danced about ere again I ventured
        near;
I was sick with dread, but I bravely said: "I'll just take a peep
        inside.
I guess he's cooked, and it's time I looked"; . . . then the door
        I opened wide.

And there sat Sam, looking cool and calm, in the heart of the
        furnace roar;

And he wore a smile you could see a mile, and he said: "Please
     close that door.
It's fine in here, but I greatly fear you'll let in the cold and
     storm—
Since I left Plumtree, down in Tennessee, it's the first time I've
     been warm."

> *There are strange things done in the midnight sun*
>   *By the men who moil for gold;*
> *The Arctic trails have their secret tales*
>   *That would make your blood run cold;*
> *The Northern Lights have seen queer sights,*
>   *But the queerest they ever did see*
> *Was that night on the marge of Lake Lebarge*
>   *I cremated Sam McGee.*

—ROBERT SERVICE

Lobster

A shoe with legs,
a stone dropped from heaven,
he does his mournful work alone,
he is like the old prospector for gold,
with secret dreams of God-heads and fish heads.
Until suddenly a cradle fastens round him
and he is trapped as the U.S.A. sleeps.
Somewhere far off a woman lights a cigarette;
somewhere far off a car goes over a bridge;
somewhere far off a bank is held up.
This is the world the lobster knows not of.
He is the old hunting dog of the sea
who in the morning will rise from it
and be undrowned
and they will take his perfect green body
and paint it red.

—ANNE SEXTON

Ozymandias

I met a traveler from an antique land
Who said: Two vast and trunkless legs of stone
Stand in the desert....Near them, on the sand,
Half sunk, a shattered visage lies, whose frown,
And wrinkled lip, and sneer of cold command,
Tell that its sculptor well those passions read
Which yet survive, stamped on these lifeless things,
The hand that mocked them, and the heart that fed:
And on the pedestal these words appear:
"My name is Ozymandias, king of kings:
Look on my works, ye Mighty, and despair!"
Nothing beside remains. Round the decay
Of that colossal wreck, boundless and bare
The lone and level sands stretch far away.

—PERCY BYSSHE SHELLEY

Sick

"I cannot go to school today,"
Said little Peggy Ann McKay.
"I have the measles and the mumps,
A gash, a rash and purple bumps.
My mouth is wet, my throat is dry,
I'm going blind in my right eye.
My tonsils are as big as rocks,
I've counted sixteen chicken pox
And there's one more—that's seventeen,
And don't you think my face looks green?
My leg is cut, my eyes are blue—
It might be instamatic flu.
I cough and sneeze and gasp and choke,
I'm sure that my left leg is broke—
My hip hurts when I move my chin,
My belly button's caving in,
My back is wrenched, my ankle's sprained,
My 'pendix pains each time it rains.
My nose is cold, my toes are numb,
I have a sliver in my thumb.
My neck is stiff, my voice is weak,
I hardly whisper when I speak.
My tongue is filling up my mouth,
I think my hair is falling out.
My elbow's bent, my spine ain't straight,
My temperature is one-o-eight.
My brain is shrunk, I cannot hear,
There is a hole inside my ear.
I have a hangnail, and my heart is—what?
What's that? What's that you say?
You say today is . . . Saturday?
G'bye, I'm going out to play!"

—SHEL SILVERSTEIN

Stone

Go inside a stone
That would be my way.
Let somebody else become a dove
Or gnash with a tiger's tooth.
I am happy to be a stone.

From the outside the stone is a riddle:
No one knows how to answer it.
Yet within, it must be cool and quiet
Even though a cow steps on it full weight,
Even though a child throws it in a river;
The stone sinks, slow, unperturbed
To the river bottom
Where the fishes come to knock on it
And listen.

I have seen sparks fly out
When two stones are rubbed,
So perhaps it is not dark inside after all;
Perhaps there is a moon shining
From somewhere, as though behind a hill—
Just enough light to make out
The strange writings, the star-charts
On the inner walls.

—CHARLES SIMIC

Great Infirmities

Everyone has only one leg.
So difficult to get around,
So difficult to climb the stairs
Without a cane or a crutch to our name.

And only one arm. Impossible contortions
Just to embrace the one you love,
To cut the bread on the table,
To put a coat on in a hurry.

I should mention that we are almost blind,
And a little deaf in both ears.
Perilous to be on the street
Among the congregations of the afflicted.

With only a few steps committed to memory,
Meekly we let ourselves be diverted
In the endless twilight—
Blind seeing-eye dogs on our leashes.

An immense stillness everywhere
With the trees always bare,
The raindrops coming down only halfway,
Coming so close and giving up.

—CHARLES SIMIC

A Theory

If a cuckoo comes into the village
Of cuckoos to cuckoo and it's Monday,
And all the cuckoos should be outdoors working,
But instead there's no one anywhere

At home, or on the road overgrown with weeds,
Or even at the little gray schoolhouse,
Oh then, the cuckoo who came to the village
Of cuckoos to cuckoo must cuckoo alone.

—CHARLES SIMIC

Fork

This strange thing must have crept
Right out of hell.
It resembles a bird's foot
Worn around the cannibal's neck.

As you hold it in your hand,
As you stab with it into a piece of meat,
It is possible to imagine the rest of the bird:
Its head which like your fist
Is large, bald, beakless and blind.

—CHARLES SIMIC

For I will consider my Cat Jeoffry
from Jubilate Agno, V

. . . For I will consider my Cat Jeoffry.

For he is the servant of the Living God duly and daily serving him.

For at the first glance of the glory of God in the East he worships
in his way.

For is this done by wreathing his body seven times round with
elegant quickness.

For then he leaps up to catch the musk, which is the blessing of
God upon his prayer.

For he rolls upon prank to work it in.

For having done duty and received blessing he begins to consider
himself.

For this he performs in ten degrees.

For first he looks upon his fore-paws to see if they are clean.

For secondly he kicks up behind to clear away there.

For thirdly he works it upon stretch with the fore-paws extended.

For fourthly he sharpens his paws by wood.

For fifthly he washes himself.

For sixthly he rolls upon wash.

For seventhly he fleas himself, that he may not be interrupted upon
the beat.

For eighthly he rubs himself against a post.

For ninthly he looks up for his instructions.

For tenthly he goes in quest of food.

For having considered God and himself he will consider his
neighbour.

For if he meets another cat he will kiss her in kindness.

For when he takes his prey he plays with it to give it chance.

For one mouse in seven escapes by his dallying.

For when his day's work is done his business more properly
begins.

For he keeps the Lord's watch in the night against the adversary.

For he counteracts the powers of darkness by his electrical skin
and glaring eyes.

For he counteracts the Devil, who is death, by brisking about the
life.

For in his morning orisons he loves the sun and the sun loves him.

For he is of the tribe of Tiger.

For the Cherub Cat is a term of the Angel Tiger.

For he has the subtlety and hissing of a serpent, which in goodness
he suppresses.

For he will not do destruction, if he is well-fed, neither will he spit
without provocation.

For he purrs in thankfulness, when God tells him he's a good Cat.

For he is an instrument for the children to learn benevolence upon.

For every house is incompleat without him and a blessing is
lacking in the spirit.

For the Lord commanded Moses concerning the cats at the
departure of the Children of Israel from Egypt.

For every family had one cat at least in the bag.

For the English Cats are the best in Europe.

For he is the cleanest in the use of his fore-paws of any
quadrupede.

For the dexterity of his defence is an instance of the love of God to
him exceedingly.

For he is the quickest to his mark of any creature.

For he is tenacious of his point.

For he is a mixture of gravity and waggery.

For he knows that God is his Saviour.

For there is nothing sweeter than his peace when at rest.

For there is nothing brisker than his life when in motion.

For he is of the Lord's poor and so indeed is he called by
benevolence perpetually— Poor Jeoffry! poor Jeoffry! the
rat has bit thy throat.

For I bless the name of the Lord Jesus that Jeoffry is better.

For the divine spirit comes about his body to sustain it in compleat
cat.

For his tonque is exceeding pure so that it has in purity what it
wants in musick.

For he is docile and can learn certain things.

For he can set up with gravity which is patience upon
approbation.

For he can fetch and carry, which is patience in employment.

For he can jump over a stick which is patience upon proof
positive.

For he can spraggle upon waggle at the word of command.
For he can jump from an eminence into his master's bosom.
For he can catch the cork and toss it again.
For he is hated by the hypocrite and miser.
For the former is afraid of detection.
For the latter refuses the charge.
For he camels his back to bear the first notion of business.
For he is good to think on, if a man would express himself neatly.
For he made a great figure in Egypt for his signal services.
For he killed the Ichneumon-rat very pernicious by land.
For his ears are so acute that they sting again.
For from this proceeds the passing quickness of his attention.
For by stroaking of him I have found out electricity.
For I perceived God's light about him both wax and fire.
For the Electrical fire is the spiritual substance, which God sends
  from heaven to sustain the bodies both of man and beast.
For God has blessed him in the variety of his movements.
For, though he cannot fly, he is an excellent clamberer.
For his motions upon the face of the earth are more than any other
  quadrupede.
For he can tread to all the measures upon the musick.
For he can swim for life.
For he can creep.

            —CHRISTOPHER SMART

Thirteen Ways of Looking
at a Blackbird

1

Among twenty snowy mountains,
The only moving thing
Was the eye of the blackbird.

2

I was of three minds,
Like a tree
In which there are three blackbirds.

3

The blackbird whirled in the autumn winds.
It was a small part of the pantomime.

4

A man and a woman
Are one.
A man and a woman and a blackbird
Are one.

5

I do not know which to prefer,
The beauty of inflections
Or the beauty of innuendoes,
The blackbird whistling
Or just after.

6

Icicles filled the long window
With barbaric glass.
The shadow of the blackbird

Crossed it, to and fro.
The mood
Traced in the shadow
An indecipherable cause.

7

O thin men of Haddam,
Why do you imagine golden birds?
Do you not see how the blackbird
Walks around the feet
Of the women about you?

8

I know noble accents
And lucid, inescapable rhythms;
But I know, too,
That the blackbird is involved
In what I know.

9

When the blackbird flew out of sight,
It marked the edge
Of one of many circles.

10

At the sight of blackbirds
Flying in a green light,
Even the bawds of euphony
Would cry out sharply.

11

He rode over Connecticut
In a glass coach.

Once, a fear pierced him,
In that he mistook
The shadow of his equipage
For blackbirds.

12

The river is moving.
The blackbird must be flying.

13

It was evening all afternoon.
It was snowing
And it was going to snow.
The blackbird sat
In the cedar-limbs.

—WALLACE STEVENS

Disillusionment of Ten O'Clock

The houses are haunted
By white night-gowns.
None are green,
Or purple with green rings,
Or green with yellow rings,
Or yellow with blue rings.
None of them are strange,
With socks of lace
And beaded ceintures.
People are not going
To dream of baboons and periwinkles.
Only, here and there, an old sailor,
Drunk and asleep in his boots,
Catches tigers
In red weather.

—WALLACE STEVENS

Good and Bad Children

Children, you are very little,
And your bones are very brittle;
If you would grow great and stately,
You must try to walk sedately.

You must still be bright and quiet,
And content with simple diet;
And remain, through all bewild'ring,
Innocent and honest children.

Happy hearts and happy faces,
Happy play in grassy places—
That was how, in ancient ages,
Children grew to kings and sages.

But the unkind and the unruly,
And the sort who eat unduly,
They must never hope for glory—
Theirs is quite a different story!

Cruel children, crying babies,
All grow up as geese and gabies,
Hated, as their age increases,
By their nephews and their nieces.

—ROBERT LOUIS STEVENSON

The Land of Story Books

At evening when the lamp is lit,
Around the fire my parents sit;
They sit at home and talk and sing,
And do not play at anything.

Now, with my little gun, I crawl
All in the dark along the wall,
And follow round the forest track
Away behind the sofa back.

There, in the night, where none can spy,
All in my hunter's camp I lie,
And play at books that I have read
Till it is time to go to bed.

These are the hills, these are the woods,
These are my starry solitudes;
And there the river by whose brink
The roaring lions come to drink.

I see the others far away
As if in firelit camp they lay,
And I, like to an Indian scout,
Around their party prowled about.

So, when my nurse comes in for me,
Home I return across the sea,
And go to bed with backward looks
At my dear Land of Story Books.

—ROBERT LOUIS STEVENSON

My Shadow

I have a little shadow that goes in and out with me,
And what can be the use of him is more than I can see.
He is very, very like me from the heels up to the head;
And I see him jump before me, when I jump into my bed.

The funniest thing about him is the way he likes to grow—
Not at all like proper children, which is always very slow;
For he sometimes shoots up taller like an India-rubber ball,
And he sometimes gets so little that there's none of him at all.

He hasn't got a notion of how children ought to play,
And can only make a fool of me in every sort of way.
He stays so close beside me, he's a coward you can see;
I'd think shame to stick to nursie as that shadow sticks to me!

One morning, very early, before the sun was up,
I rose and found the shining dew on every buttercup;
But my lazy little shadow, like an arrant sleepyhead,
Had stayed at home behind me and was fast asleep in bed.

—ROBERT LOUIS STEVENSON

The Land of Counterpane

When I was sick and lay a-bed,
I had two pillows at my head,
And all my toys beside me lay
To keep me happy all the day.

And sometimes for an hour or so
I watched my leaden soldiers go,
With different uniforms and drills,
Among the bed-clothes, through the hills;

And sometimes sent my ships in fleets
All up and down among the sheets;
Or brought my trees and houses out,
And planted cities all about.

I was the giant great and still
That sits upon the pillow-hill,
And sees before him, dale and plain,
The pleasant land of counterpane.

—ROBERT LOUIS STEVENSON

The Swing

How do you like to go up in a swing,
Up in the air so blue?
Oh, I do think it is the pleasantest thing
Ever a child can do!

Up in the air and over the wall,
Till I can see so wide,
River and trees and cattle and all
Over the countryside—

Till I look down on the garden green,
Down on the roof so brown—
Up in the air I go flying again,
Up in the air and down!

—ROBERT LOUIS STEVENSON

Twinkle Twinkle Little Star

Twinkle, twinkle, little star,
How I wonder what you are!
Up above the world so high,
Like a diamond in the sky.

When the blazing sun is gone,
When he nothing shines upon,
Then you show your little light,
Twinkle, twinkle all the night.

Then the traveller in the dark,
Thanks you for your tiny spark,
He could not see which way to go
If you did not twinkle so.

In the dark blue sky you keep,
And often through my curtains peep,
For you never shut your eye,
'Til the sun is in the sky.

As your bright and tiny spark
Lights the traveller in the dark—
Though I know not what you are,
Twinkle, twinkle, little star.

—JANE TAYLOR

The Falling Star

I saw a star slide down the sky,
Blinding the north as it went by,
Too burning and too quick to hold,
Too lovely to be bought or sold,
Good only to make wishes on
And then forever to be gone.

— SARA TEASDALE

The Eagle

He clasps the crag with crooked hands;
Close to the sun in lonely lands,
Ringed with the azure world, he stands.

The wrinkled sea beneath him crawls;
He watches from his mountain walls,
And like a thunderbolt he falls.

—ALFRED, LORD TENNYSON

Charge of the Light Brigade

Half a league, half a league,
Half a league onward,
All in the valley of Death
  Rode the six hundred.
"Forward, the Light Brigade!
Charge for the guns!" he said:
Into the valley of Death
  Rode the six hundred.

"Forward, the Light Brigade!"
Was there a man dismayed?
Not tho' the soldiers knew
  Someone had blundered:
Theirs not to make reply,
Theirs not to reason why,
Theirs but to do and die:
Into the valley of Death
  Rode the six hundred.

Cannon to right of them,
Cannon to left of them,
Cannon in front of them
  Volleyed and thunder'd;
Storm'd at with shot and shell,
Boldly they rode and well,
Into the jaws of Death,
Into the mouth of Hell,
  Rode the six hundred.

Flashed all their sabres bare,
Flashed as they turned in air,
Sab'ring the gunners there,
Charging an army, while
  All the world wondered:
Plunged in the battery smoke,
Right through the line they broke;
Cossack and Russian
Reeled from the sabre-stroke
  Shattered and sundered.

Then they rode back, but not—
        Not the six hundred.

Cannon to right of them,
Cannon to left of them,
Cannon behind them
        Volleyed and thundered;
Stormed at with shot and shell,
While horse and hero fell,
They that had fought so well
Came thro' the jaws of Death,
Back from the mouth of Hell,
All that was left of them,
        Left of six hundred.

When can their glory fade?
Oh, the wild charge they made!
        All the world wondered.
Honor the charge they made!
Honor the Light Brigade,
        Noble Six Hundred!
                                —ALFRED, LORD TENNYSON

The Brook

I come from haunts of coot and hern,
  I make a sudden sally,
And sparkle out among the fern,
  To bicker down a valley.

By thirty hills I hurry down,
  Or slip between the ridges,
By twenty thorps, a little town,
  And half a hundred bridges.

I chatter over stony ways
  In little sharps and trebles,
I bubble into eddying bays,
  I babble on the pebbles.

With many a curve my banks I fret
  By many a field and fallow,
And many a fairy foreland set
  With willow-weed and mallow.

I chatter, chatter, as I flow
  To join the brimming river,
For men may come and men may go,
  But I go on for ever.

I wind about and in and out,
  With here a blossom sailing,
And here and there a lusty trout,
  And here and there a grayling.

And here and there a foamy flake
  Upon me, as I travel
With many a silvery waterbreak
  Above the golden gravel.

I steal by lawns and grassy plots,
  I slide by hazel covers;
I move the sweet forget-me-nots
  That grow for happy lovers.

I slip, I slide, I gloom, I glance,
  Among my skimming swallows;
I make the netted sunbeam dance
  Against my sandy shallows.

I murmur under moon and stars
  In brambly wildernesses;
I linger by my singly bars;
  I loiter round my cresses;

And out again I curve and flow
  To join the brimming river,
For men may come and men may go,
  But I go on for ever.

      —ALFRED, LORD TENNYSON

Songs

from The Princess

The splendour falls on castle walls
      And snowy summits old in story:
The long light shakes across the lakes,
      And the wild cataract leaps in glory.
Blow, bugle, blow, set the wild echoes flying,
Blow, bugle; answer, echoes, dying, dying, dying.

O hark, O hear! how thin and clear,
      And thinner, clearer, farther going!
O sweet and far from cliff and scar
      The horns of Elfland faintly blowing!
Blow, let us hear the purple glens replying:
Blow, bugle; answer, echoes, dying, dying, dying.

O love, they die in yon rich sky,
      They faint on hill or field or river:
Our echoes roll from soul to soul,
      And grow for ever and for ever.
Blow, bugle, blow, set the wild echoes flying,
And answer, echoes, answer, dying, dying, dying.

—ALFRED, LORD TENNYSON

Sweet and Low

Sweet and low, sweet and low,
    Wind of the western sea,
Low, low, breathe and blow,
    Wind of the western sea!
Over the rolling waters go,
Come from the dying moon, and blow,
    Blow him again to me;
While my little one, while my pretty one, sleeps.

Sleep and rest, sleep and rest,
    Father will come to thee soon;
Rest, rest on mother's breast,
    Father will come to thee soon;
Father will come to his babe in the nest,
Silver sails all out of the west
    Under the silver moon;
Sleep, my little one, sleep, my pretty one, sleep.

                  —ALFRED, LORD TENNYSON

Casey at the Bat

It looked extremely rocky for the Mudville nine that day;
The score stood two to four, with but one inning left to play.
So, when Cooney died at second, and Burrows did the same,
A pallor wreathed the features of the patrons of the game.

A straggling few got up to go, leaving there the rest,
With that hope which springs eternal within the human breast.
For they thought: "If only Casey could get a whack at that,"
They'd put even money now, with Casey at the bat.

But Flynn preceded Casey, and likewise so did Blake,
And the former was a pudd'n, and the latter was a fake.
So on that stricken multitude a deathlike silence sat;
For there seemed but little chance of Casey's getting to the bat.

But Flynn let drive a single, to the wonderment of all.
And the much-despised Blakey "tore the cover off the ball."
And when the dust had lifted, and they saw what had occurred,
There was Blakey safe at second, and Flynn a-huggin' third.

Then from the gladdened multitude went up a joyous yell—
It rumbled in the mountaintops, it rattled in the dell;
It struck upon the hillside and rebounded on the flat;
For Casey, mighty Casey, was advancing to the bat.

There was ease in Casey's manner as he stepped into his place,
There was pride in Casey's bearing and a smile on Casey's face;
And when responding to the cheers he lightly doffed his hat,
No stranger in the crowd could doubt 'twas Casey at the bat.

Ten thousand eyes were on him as he rubbed his hands with dirt,
Five thousand tongues applauded when he wiped them on his shirt;
Then when the writhing pitcher ground the ball into his hip,
Defiance glanced in Casey's eye, a sneer curled Casey's lip.

And now the leather-covered sphere came hurtling through the air,
And Casey stood a-watching it in haughty grandeur there.
Close by the sturdy batsman the ball unheeded sped;
"That ain't my style," said Casey. "Strike one," the umpire said.

From the benches, black with people, there went up a muffled roar,
Like the beating of the storm waves on the stern and distant shore.
"Kill him! Kill the umpire!" shouted someone in the stand;
And it's likely they'd have killed him had not Casey raised his hand.

With a smile of Christian charity great Casey's visage shone;
He stilled the rising tumult, he made the game go on;
He signaled to the pitcher, and once more the spheroid flew;
But Casey still ignored it, and the umpire said, "Strike two."

"Fraud!" cried the maddened thousands, and the echo answered "Fraud!"
But one scornful look from Casey and the audience was awed;
They saw his face grow stern and cold, they saw his muscles strain,
And they knew that Casey wouldn't let the ball go by again.

The sneer is gone from Casey's lips, his teeth are clenched in hate,
He pounds with cruel vengeance his bat upon the plate;
And now the pitcher holds the ball, and now he lets it go,
And now the air is shattered by the force of Casey's blow.

Oh, somewhere in this favored land the sun is shining bright,
The band is playing somewhere, and somewhere hearts are light;
And somewhere men are laughing, and somewhere children shout,
But there is no joy in Mudville—mighty Casey has struck out.

—ERNEST LAWRENCE THAYER

Do Not Go Gentle into That Good Night

Do not go gentle into that good night,
Old age should burn and rave at close of day;
Rage, rage against the dying of the light.

Though wise men at their end know dark is right,
Because their words had forked no lightning they
Do not go gentle into that good night.

Good men, the last wave by, crying how bright
Their frail deeds might have danced in a green bay,
Rage, rage against the dying of the light.

Wild men who caught and sang the sun in flight,
And learn, too late, they grieved it on its way,
Do not go gentle into that good night.

Grave men, near death, who see with blinding sight
Blind eyes could blaze like meteors and be gay,
Rage, rage against the dying of the light.

And you, my father, there on the sad height,
Curse, bless, me now with your fierce tears, I pray.
Do not go gentle into that good night.
Rage, rage against the dying of the light.

—DYLAN THOMAS

Fern Hill

Now as I was young and easy under the apple boughs
About the lilting house and happy as the grass was green,
    The night above the dingle starry,
        Time let me hail and climb
    Golden in the heydays of his eyes,
And honoured among wagons I was prince of the apple towns
And once below a time I lordly had the trees and leaves
        Trail with daisies and barley
    Down the rivers of the windfall light.

And as I was green and carefree, famous among the barns
About the happy yard and singing as the farm was home,
    In the sun that is young once only,
        Time let me play and be
    Golden in the mercy of his means,
And green and golden I was huntsman and herdsman, the calves
Sang to my horn, the foxes on the hills barked clear and cold,
        And the sabbath rang slowly
    In the pebbles of the holy streams.

All the sun long it was running, it was lovely, the hay
Fields high as the house, and the tunes from the chimneys, it was air
    And playing, lovely and watery
        And fire green as grass.
    And nightly under the simple stars
As I rode to sleep the owls were bearing the farm away,
All the moon long I heard, blessed among stables, the night jars
        Flying with the ricks, and the horses
        Flashing into the dark.

And then to awake, and the farm, like a wanderer white
With the dew, come back, the cock on his shoulder: it was all
    Shining, it was Adam and maiden,
        The sky gathered again
    And the sun grew round that very day.
So it must have been after the birth of the simple light

In the first, spinning place, the spellbound horses walking warm
  Out of the whinnying green stable
    On to the field of praise.

And honoured among foxes and pheasants by the gay house
Under the new made clouds and happy as the heart was long,
    In the sun born over and over,
        I ran my heedless ways,
        My wishes raced through the house high hay
And nothing I cared, at my sky blue trades, that time allows
In all his tuneful turning so few and such morning songs
    Before the children green and golden
        Follow him out of grace,

Nothing I cared, in the lamb white days, that time would take me
Up the swallow thronged loft by the shadow of my hand,
    In the moon that is always rising,
        Nor that riding to sleep
    I should hear him fly with the high fields
And wake to the farm forever fled from the childless land.
Oh as I was young and easy in the mercy of his means,
    Time held me green and dying
    Though I sang in my chains like the sea.

—DYLAN THOMAS

A Shooting Star

From Ariadne's Crown
      Something came flashing down
     Over the distant town,
    Over the river and sleeping farms;
The planets above seemed to wink
As they watched the traveler sink;
And motherly Earth, I think,
May have folded a little lost star in her arms.

                         —EDITH M. THOMAS

The Owl

Downhill I came, hungry, and yet not starved;
Cold, yet had heat within me that was proof
Against the North wind; tired, yet so that rest
Had seemed the sweetest thing under a roof.

Then at the inn I had food, fire, and rest,
Knowing how hungry, cold, and tired was I.
All of the night was quite barred out except
An owl's cry, a most melancholy cry

Shaken out long and clear upon the hill,
No merry note, nor cause of merriment,
But one telling me plain what I escaped
And others could not, that night, as in I went.

And salted was my food, and my repose,
Salted and sobered, too, by the bird's voice
Speaking for all who lay under the stars,
Soldiers and poor, unable to rejoice.

—EDWARD THOMAS

First Thanksgiving of All

Peace and Mercy and Jonathan,
And Patience (very small),
Stood by the table giving thanks
The first Thanksgiving of all.
There was very little for them to eat,
Nothing special and nothing sweet;
Only bread and a little broth,
And a bit of fruit (and no tablecloth);
But Peace and Mercy and Jonathan
And Patience, in a row,
Stood up and asked a blessing on
Thanksgiving, long ago.
Thankful they were their ship had come
Safely across the sea;
Thankful they were for hearth and home,
And kin and company;
They were glad of broth to go with their bread,
Glad their apples were round and red,
Glad of mayflowers they would bring
Out of the woods again next spring.
So Peace and Mercy and Jonathan,
And Patience (very small),
Stood up gratefully giving thanks
The first Thanksgiving of all.

—NANCY BYRD TURNER

America for Me

'Tis fine to see the Old World, and travel up and down
Among the famous palaces and cities of renown,
To admire the crumbly castles and the statues of the kings,—
But now I think I've had enough of antiquated things.

> So it's home again, and home again, America for me!
> My heart is turning home again, and there I long to be,
> In the land of youth and freedom beyond the ocean bars,
> Where the air is full of sunlight and the flag is full of stars.

Oh, London is a man's town, there's power in the air;
And Paris is a woman's town, with flowers in her hair;
And it's sweet to dream in Venice, and it's great to study Rome;
But when it comes to living there is no place like home.

I like the German fir-woods, in green battalions drilled;
I like the gardens of Versailles with flashing fountains filled;
But, oh, to take your hand, my dear, and ramble for a day
In the friendly western woodland where Nature has her way!

I know that Europe's wonderful, yet something seems to lack:
The Past is too much with her, and the people looking back.
But the glory of the Present is to make the Future free,—
We love our land for what she is and what she is to be.

> Oh, it's home again, and home again, America for me!
> I want a ship that's westward bound to plough the rolling sea,
> To the blessed Land of Room Enough beyond the ocean bars,
> Where the air is full of sunlight and the flag is full of stars.

—HENRY VAN DYKE

How Doth the Little Busy Bee

How doth the little busy bee
    Improve each shining hour,
And gather honey all the day
    From every opening flower!

How skillfully she builds her cell!
    How neat she spreads the wax!
And labors hard to store it well
    With the sweet food she makes.

In works of labor or of skill
    I would be busy too;
For Satan finds some mischief still
    For idle hands to do.

In books, or work, or healthful play,
    Let my first years be passed,
That I may give for every day
    Some good account at last.

—ISAAC WATTS

Chairs in Snow

Quiet upon the terraces,
    The garden chairs repose;
In fall they wore their sooty dress,
    Now the lees of snows.

How like the furnishings of youth,
    In back yards of the mind:
Residuals of summer's truth
    And seasons left behind.

—E.B. WHITE

O Captain! My Captain!

O Captain! my Captain! our fearful trip is done,
The ship has weather'd every rack, the prize we sought is won,
    The port is near, the bells I hear, the people all exulting,
    While follow eyes the steady keel, the vessel grim and
        daring;

        But O heart! heart! heart!
           O the bleeding drops of red,
       Where on the deck my Captain lies,
         Fallen cold and dead.

O Captain! my Captain! rise up and hear the bells;
Rise up—for you the flag is flung—for you the bugle trills,
    For you bouquets and ribbon'd wreaths—for you the
        shores a-crowding,
    For you they call, the swaying mass, their eager faces
        turning;

        Here, Captain! dear father!
           This arm beneath your head!
       It is some dream that on the deck,
         You've fallen cold and dead.

My Captain does not answer, his lips are pale and still,
My father does not feel my arm, he has no pulse nor will,
    The ship is anchor'd safe and sound, its voyage closed and
        done,
    From fearful trip the victor ship comes in with object won;

        Exult, O shores! and ring, O bells!
           But I with mournful tread,
       Walk the deck my Captain lies,
         Fallen cold and dead.

—WALT WHITMAN

When I Heard the Learn'd Astronomer

When I heard the learn'd astronomer,
When the proofs, the figures, were ranged in columns before me,
When I was shown the charts and diagrams, to add, divide, and
     measure them,
When I sitting heard the astronomer where he lectured with
     much applause in the lecture-room,
How soon unaccountable I became tired and sick,
Till rising and gliding out I wander'd off by myself,
In the mystical moist night-air, and from time to time,
Look'd up in perfect silence at the stars.

                      —WALT WHITMAN

Barbara Frietchie

Up from the meadows rich with corn,
Clear in the cool September morn,

The clustered spires of Frederick stand
Green-walled by the hills of Maryland

Round about them orchards sweep,
Apple and peach tree fruited deep,

Fair as the garden of the Lord
To the eyes of the famished rebel horde,

On that pleasant morn of the early fall
When Lee marched over the mountain-wall;

Over the mountains winding down
Horse and foot, into Frederick town.

Forty flags with their silver stars,
Forty flags with their crimson bars,

Flapped in the morning wind; the sun
Of noon looked down and saw not one.

Up rose old Barbara Frietchie then,
Bowed with her fourscore years and ten;

Bravest of all in Frederick town,
She took up the flag the men hauled down;

In her attic window the staff she set,
To show that one heart was loyal yet.

Up the street came the rebel tread,
Stonewall Jackson riding ahead.

Under his slouched hat left and right
He glanced; the old flag met his sight.

"Halt!"—the dust-brown ranks stood fast.
"Fire!"—out blazed the rifle-blast.

It shivered the window, pane and sash;
It rent the banner with seam and gash.

Quick, as it fell, from the broken staff
Dame Barbara snatched the silken scarf.

She leaned far out on the window-sill,
And shook it forth with a royal will.

"Shoot, if you must, this old gray head,
But spare your country's flag," she said.

A shade of sadness, a blush of shame,
Over the face of the leader came;

The nobler nature within him stirred
To life at that woman's deed and word;

"Who touches a hair of yon gray head
Dies like a dog! March on!" he said.

All day long through Frederick street
Sounded the tread of marching feet:

All day long that free flag tossed
Over the heads of the rebel host.

Ever its torn folds rose and fell
On the loyal winds that loved it well;

And through the hill-gaps sunset light
Shone over it with a warm good-night.

Barbara Frietchie's work is o'er,
And the Rebel rides on his raids no more.

Honor to her! and let a tear
Fall, for her sake, on Stonewall's bier.

Over Barbara Frietchie's grave,
Flag of Freedom and Union, wave!

Peace and order and beauty draw
Round thy symbol of light and law;

And ever the stars above look down
On the stars below in Frederick town!

—JOHN GREENLEAF WHITTIER

This Is Just to Say

I have eaten
the plums
that were in
the icebox

and which
you were probably
saving
for breakfast

Forgive me
they were delicious
so sweet
and so cold

—WILLIAM CARLOS WILLIAMS

Poem

As the cat
climbed over
the top of

the jamcloset
first the right
forefoot

carefully
then the hind
stepped down

into the pit of
the empty
flowerpot

—WILLIAM CARLOS WILLIAMS

The Red Wheelbarrow

so much depends
upon

a red wheel
barrow

glazed with rain
water

beside the white
chickens

—WILLIAM CARLOS WILLIAMS

Spring and All

By the road to the contagious hospital
under the surge of the blue
mottled clouds driven from the
northeast—cold wind. Beyond, the
waste of broad, muddy fields
brown with dried weeds, standing and fallen

patches of standing water
the scattering of tall trees

All along the road the reddish
purplish, forked, upstanding, twiggy
stuff of bushes and small trees
with dead, brown leaves under them
leafless vines—

Lifeless in appearance, sluggish
dazed spring approaches—

They enter the new world naked,
cold, uncertain of all
save that they enter. All about them
the cold, familiar wind—

Now the grass, tomorrow
the stiff curl of wildcarrot leaf
One by one objects are defined—
It quickens: clarity, outline of leaf

But now the stark dignity of
entrance—Still, the profound change
has come upon them: rooted, they
grip down and begin to awaken

—WILLIAM CARLOS WILLIAMS

When I Grow Up

When I grow up,
I think I'll be
A detective
With a skeleton key.

I could be a soldier
And a sailor too;
I'd like to be a keeper
At the public zoo.

I'll own a trumpet
And I'll play a tune;
I'll keep a space ship
To explore the moon.

I'll be a cowboy
And live in the saddle;
I'll be a guide
With a canoe and a paddle.

I'd like to be the driver
On a diesel train;
And it must be fun
To run a building crane.

I'll live in a lighthouse
And guard the shore;
And I know I'll want to be
A dozen things more.

For the more a boy lives
The more a boy learns—
I think I'll be all of them
By taking turns.

—WILLIAM WISE

Choosing Shoes

New shoes, new shoes,
 Red and pink and blue shoes.
Tell me, what would *you* choose,
 If they'd let us buy?

Buckle shoes, bow shoes,
 Pretty pointy-toe shoes,
Strappy, cappy low shoes;
 Let's have some to try.

Bright shoes, white shoes,
 Dandy-dance-by-night shoes,
Perhaps-a-little-tight shoes,
 Like some? So would I.

 But

Flat shoes, fat shoes,
 Stump-along-like-that shoes,
Wipe-them-on-the-mat shoes,
 That's the sort they'll buy.

—FFRIDA WOLFE

Written in March

While Resting on the Bridge at the Foot
of Brother's Water

The cock is crowing,
The stream is flowing,
The small birds twitter,
The lake doth glitter,
The green field sleeps in the sun;
The oldest and youngest
Are at work with the strongest;
The cattle are grazing,
Their heads never raising;
There are forty feeding like one!

Like an army defeated
The snow hath retreated,
And now doth fare ill
On the top of the bare hill;
The ploughboy is whooping—anon—anon:
There's joy in the mountains;
There's life in the fountains;
Small clouds are sailing,
Blue sky prevailing;
The rain is over and gone!

—WILLIAM WORDSWORTH

My Heart Leaps Up When I Behold

My heart leaps up when I behold
    A rainbow in the sky;
So was it when my life began;
So it is now I am a man;
So be it when I shall grow old,
    Or let me die!
The Child is father of the Man;
And I could wish my days to be
Bound each to each by natural piety.

—WILLIAM WORDSWORTH

Composed upon Westminster Bridge

September 3, 1802

Earth has not anything to show more fair:
Dull would he be of soul who could pass by
A sight so touching in its majesty:
This City now doth, like a garment, wear
The beauty of the morning: silent, bare,
Ships, towers, domes, theatres, and temples lie
Open unto the fields, and to the sky;
All bright and glittering in the smokeless air.
Never did sun more beautifully steep
In his first splendor, valley, rock, or hill;
Ne'er saw I, never felt, a calm so deep!
The river glideth at his own sweet will:
Dear God! the very houses seem asleep;
And all that mighty heart is lying still!

—WILLIAM WORDSWORTH

Daffodils

I wandered lonely as a cloud
     That floats on high o'er vales and hills,
When all at once I saw a crowd,
     A host, of golden daffodils;
Beside the lake, beneath the trees,
     Fluttering and dancing in the breeze.

Continuous as the stars that shine
     And twinkle on the Milky Way,
They stretched in never-ending line
     Along the margin of a bay;
Ten thousand saw I at a glance,
     Tossing their heads in sprightly dance.

The waves beside them danced, but they
     Outdid the sparkling waves in glee.
A poet could not but be gay,
     In such a jocund company!
I gazed, and gazed, but little thought
     What wealth the show to me had brought;

For oft, when on my couch I lie
     In vacant or in pensive mood,
They flash upon that inward eye
     Which is the bliss of solitude;
And then my heart with pleasure fills,
     And dances with the daffodils.

—WILLIAM WORDSWORTH

The Kitten at Play

See the kitten on the wall,
Sporting with the leaves that fall,
Withered leaves, one, two and three
Falling from the elder tree,
Through the calm and frosty air
Of the morning bright and fair.

See the kitten, how she starts,
Crouches, stretches, paws and darts;
With a tiger-leap half way
Now she meets her coming prey.
Lets it go as fast and then
Has it in her power again.

Now she works with three and four,
Like an Indian conjurer;
Quick as he in feats of art,
Gracefully she plays her part;
Yet were gazing thousands there;
What would little Tabby care?

—WILLIAM WORDSWORTH

A Blessing

Just off the highway to Rochester, Minnesota,
Twilight bounds softly forth on the grass.
And the eyes of those two Indian ponies
Darken with kindness.
They have come gladly out of the willows
To welcome my friend and me.
We step over the barbed wire into the pasture
Where they have been grazing all day, alone.
They ripple tensely, they can hardly contain their happiness
That we have come.
They bow shyly as wet swans. They love each other.
There is no loneliness like theirs.
At home once more,
They begin munching the young tufts of spring in the darkness.
I would like to hold the slenderer one in my arms,
For she has walked over to me
And nuzzled my left hand.
She is black and white,
Her mane falls wild on her forehead,
And the light breeze moves me to caress her long ear
That is delicate as the skin over a girl's wrist.
Suddenly I realize
That if I stepped out of my body I would break
Into blossom.

—JAMES WRIGHT

Escape

When foxes eat the last gold grape,
And the last white antelope is killed,
I shall stop fighting and escape
Into a little house I'll build.

But first I'll shrink to fairy size,
With a whisper no one understands,
Making blind moons of all your eyes,
And muddy roads of all your hands.

And you may grope for me in vain
In hollows under the mangrove root,
Or where, in apple-scented rain,
The silver wasp-nests hang like fruit.

—ELINOR WYLIE

The Lake Isle of Innisfree

I will arise and go now, and go to Innisfree,
And a small cabin build there, of clay and wattles made:
Nine bean-rows will I have there, a hive for the honey-bee,
And live alone in the bee-loud glade.

And I shall have some peace there, for peace comes dropping slow,
Dropping from the veils of the morning to where the cricket sings;
There midnight's all a glimmer, and noon a purple glow,
And evening full of the linnet's wings.

I will arise and go now, for always night and day
I hear lake water lapping with low sounds by the shore;
While I stand on the roadway, or on the pavements gray,
I hear it in the deep heart's core.

—WILLIAM BUTLER YEATS

To a Squirrel at Kyle-Na-No

Come play with me;
Why should you run
Through the shaking tree
As though I'd a gun
To strike you dead?
When all I would do
Is to scratch your head
And let you go.

—WILLIAM BUTLER YEATS

The Song of Wandering Aengus

I went out to the hazel wood,
Because a fire was in my head,
And cut and peeled a hazel wand,
And hooked a berry to a thread;
And when white moths were on the wing,
And moth-like stars were flickering out,
I dropped the berry in a stream,
And caught a little silver trout.

When I had laid it on the floor
I went to blow the fire aflame,
But something rustled on the floor,
And someone called me by my name;
It had become a glimmering girl
With apple blossom in her hair
Who called me by my name and ran
And faded through the brightening air.

Though I am old with wandering
Through hollow lands and hilly lands,
I will find out where she has gone,
And kiss her lips and take her hands;
And walk among long dappled grass,
And pluck till time and times are done
The silver apples of the moon,
The golden apples of the sun.

—WILLIAM BUTLER YEATS

An Irish Airman Foresees His Death

I know that I shall meet my fate
Somewhere among the clouds above;
Those that I fight I do not hate,
Those that I guard I do not love;
My country is Kiltartan Cross,
My countrymen Kiltartan's poor,
No likely end could bring them loss
Or leave them happier than before.
Nor law, nor duty bade me fight,
Nor public men, nor cheering crowds,
A lonely impulse of delight
Drove to this tumult in the clouds;
I balanced all, brought all to mind,
The years to come seemed waste of breath,
A waste of breath the years behind
In balance with this life, this death.

—WILLIAM BUTLER YEATS

He Wishes for the Cloths of Heaven

Had I the heavens' embroidered cloths,
Enwrought with golden and silver light,
The blue and the dim and the dark cloths
Of night and light and the half light,
I would spread the cloths under your feet:
But I, being poor, have only my dreams;
I have spread my dreams under your feet;
Tread softly because you tread on my dreams.

—WILLIAM BUTLER YEATS

Epitaph for a Concord Boy

Now there is none of the living who can remember
How quietly the sun came into the village of Concord,
No one who will know of the sun in the eyes of the dead boy
There on the village green, where he fell.

He did not fall because he hated the Redcoats,
Indeed, he would have known little of them
Had not that quick, grim man, his father,
Hurried him dutifully toward the crackle of musketry.

His father had routed him out and stuck a gun in his hand
And then said something about the "country's deliverance,"
Until the boy went, rubbing the dreams from his eyes
And stood on the green with the others, facing the soldiers.

When the Redcoat leader had shouted, "Disperse, ye rebels,"
The boy would have gone back to his bed willingly,
But as no one else went, he stayed, watching the elegant enemy.
He was never aware the volley of war had been sounded.

Shot through the heart he took less time to die
Than the rabbits he had himself killed, many a day.
Though when his tight hand clutched at his own blood
It was as if he had never met death, entirely.

Once, for a split second, he wondered
Why he could not raise his strong legs from the grass,
And why the slow granite of his father's face
Was melting above him, for it never had.

He would have spoken now to his father, but the words were not
     there.
Plainly the thoughts for his tongue were bound in his plow-taut
     hands,
In the fields out of Concord he had said what he could with them,
And now when his heart grew dark, he was left with no other
     words.

—STANLEY YOUNG

COPYRIGHT ACKNOWLEDGMENTS

INDEX OF POEMS